ALSO BY STEWART GILES:

THE DS JASON SMITH SERIES –
- 1. Smith
- 2. Boomerang
- 3. Ladybird
- 4. Occam's Razor
- 5. Harlequin
- 6. Selene
- 7. Horsemen
- 8. Unworthy
- Prequel. Phobia

THE DC HARRIET TAYLOR SERIES -
- 1. The Beekeeper
- 2. The Perfect Murder
- 3. The Backpacker

2

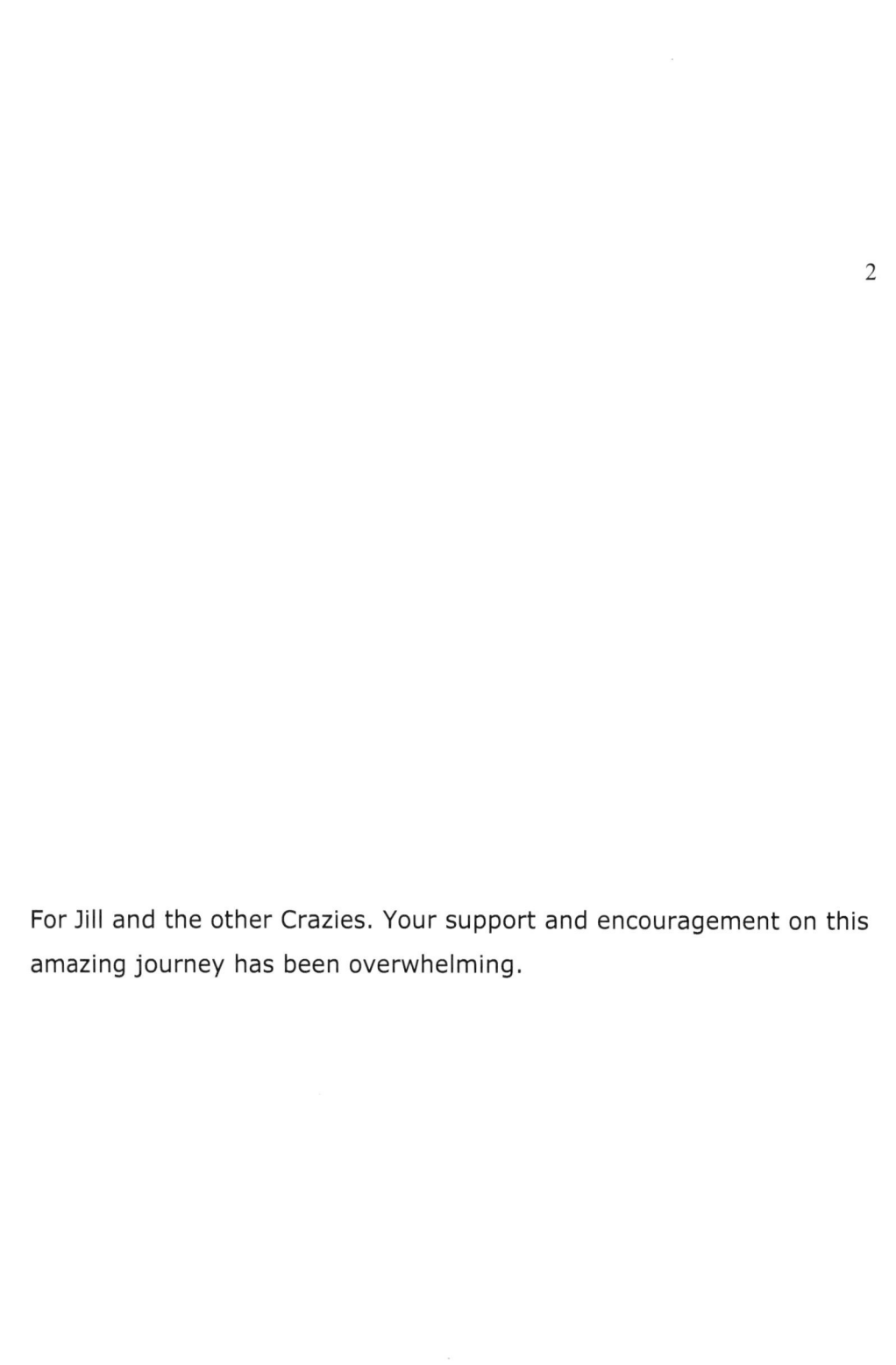

For Jill and the other Crazies. Your support and encouragement on this amazing journey has been overwhelming.

GLOSSARY OF NAUTICAL TERMS:

Block – A pulley that makes it easier to pull in and release the ropes.
Boom – A vertical spar that attaches to the main sail.
Boom Vang – A sail control that allows one to make downward tension on the boom.
Cleat – A stationary device that is used to secure a rope.
Foresail - The sail at the front of the boat.
Furler – A device that allows the foresail to be hoisted and dropped from the cockpit.
Gybe preventer – A system to prevent accidental turning of the vessel.
Halyard – A rope attached to the sail to enable it to be hoisted.
Helm – A vessel's steering mechanism.
Hull speed – The maximum efficient speed of a vessel.
Jib sheet – A line on either side of the boat used to control the foresail.
Knot – A unit of speed. 1 nautical mile – 1.8520km.
Mainsail – The sail attached to the boom.
Mainsheet – A sail control to change the angle of the boom, thus controlling the shape of the mainsail.
Painter – A rope used to secure the vessel to a jetty.

1996

She ran. She ran like her life depended on it.
It probably did.

She could hear his breathing behind her – steady breaths that sounded in time with his footsteps. He was getting closer, and she pushed herself some more. She could see the smoke coming out of the chimney in the old farmhouse far in the distance. The smoke was going straight up – there wasn't a breath of wind in the air. She thought she could feel *his* breath on her neck. The farmhouse didn't seem to be getting any closer.

I'm not going to make it. This is what it feels like to know you're about to die.

He was getting closer, and the farmhouse was too far away. The fields were empty. She felt a hand on her back, he screamed something in a language she didn't understand and then she was free. She carried on running. The footsteps behind her were gone. She glanced back as she ran. He'd tripped and fallen and was picking himself up off the ground.

She reached the farmhouse and banged on the door. As she waited for it to open she scanned the field. Her pursuer was gone.

CHAPTER ONE

Carrion. That's what the jackdaws could pick up in the breeze – the scent of carrion. The rooks had got there first. Scores of them, their wings beating in a frenzy of excitement. This kill was theirs. The crows waited in the sidelines. They were next in line. The jackdaws would have to be content with the scraps. One of the rooks pecked at something hard and recoiled, stunned. Their meal had been partially hidden between a pile of rocks on the far side of Landell's farm. A heap of dead branches had been placed on top, but the full force of an Atlantic South-Westerly during the night had lifted most of them off. Now, the smell of carrion had drawn scavengers from far and wide.

It was the mob of birds that had caught the eye of Gilly Landell. Gilly was the wife of William Landell Junior, the owner of the farm. By the time she'd spotted the feeding frenzy there were more than fifty birds hanging around the scene. Gilly's first thought was that a sheep had perished in the night. It was lambing season, and the lambs were especially vulnerable. Foxes were becoming more and more of a nuisance on the farm. She started up the quad bike and made her way through the field towards the squawking rabble.

The crows and the jackdaws took flight as she approached, as did the majority of the rooks. A few of the bold ones stood their ground – this feast was theirs and they weren't going to give it up without a fight. Gilly Landell stopped the quad bike and got off. She shooed the remaining birds away and moved in to take a closer look at what had attracted them to the far edge of the farm in the first place.

Gilly could see straight away that it wasn't a sheep the birds were interested in. The branches that had blown off during the night revealed the body of a young woman. Her blonde hair was matted with blood. Gilly was well accustomed to death – growing up on a farm meant that death was a part of life but the body of the young woman lying amongst the rocks was something she wouldn't forget for a very long time. One of her blue eyes was open. The other one was gone – bird food. The blood in the empty socket was black. Gilly Landell turned to one side and vomited on the rocks.

CHAPTER TWO

The Wandering Albatross was in her element. A steady twenty knot blow was pushing Dr Jon Finch's Westerly 26 as close to hull speed as Finch had ever dared to push her before.
"You can ease off on the sheet a bit if you like," he had to shout over the din of the wind on the sails. "She won't go any faster, you know." Harriet Taylor reluctantly let out the Jib sheet and the boat levelled out slightly.

The sailing bug had bitten DC Harriet hard. Ever since she'd first set foot on Jon's boat, six months earlier, she'd been well and truly hooked. Harriet and Jon had spent the night out on the boat. They'd anchored out about four nautical miles as the crow flies from the marina in Trotterdown, and now they were heading back in.

"I'll make us some more coffee," Jon peeled his hands off the wheel. His knuckles were white. "Cleat the Jib sheet and take over."
"Yes, Captain." Harriet pulled the rope tighter and slotted it inside the cleat. She kissed him on the forehead and moved aside so he could ease his six-foot eight frame inside the cabin.
She took hold of the wheel, pulled in the main sheet and bore off a few degrees. She smiled as the speed indicator registered an increase of half a knot.

Jon emerged with two steaming mugs off coffee and slotted them both into the cup holders on the starboard side.
"That was quite a night," he said. "I reckon we got hit by some forty-plus gusters last night."
Harriet locked the wheel and the boat held her course.
"I should've done this years ago," she picked up the coffee and warmed her hands on the mug.

It was early March, winter was a distant memory, but it was still quite chilly in the breeze.
"I've never seen anybody take to it so quickly," Jon said. "You've got no fear."
"What's to fear? You're always bragging about how stable the Albatross is."
　　Jon unlocked the wheel and took the helm again. He eased off on the mainsheet, and the boat became easier to handle.
"You scare me sometimes, Harriet."
"I scare you?"
"The Westerly 26 is a cruising boat. She was designed as a safe, easy to handle family cruiser - a peaceful, slow water boat. You sail her like you're racing the Sydney to Hobart sometimes."
Harriet didn't know how to react to this. She wasn't sure whether to be offended or complimented. She opted for the latter.
"Well, now you've been educated on what this tub is actually capable of. It's exhilarating."
Jon smiled. Harriet was right. His sailing trips had become infinitely more enjoyable with her on board.
　　"Are we going in?" Harriet took the empty coffee mugs down below and stowed them in the gimbaled sink.
"I have a management meeting at eleven," Jon replied. "I want to have a quick shower and change my clothes before I head to the hospital. What about you?"
"I have a rare day off. I was thinking about maybe messing around on the boat for a few hours. In the marina, I mean. There's a few things I've noticed that need fixing up."
"You're not going to girlify her, are you? If there is such a word."

"Girlify? Good God, no. There are some ropes and fittings down below that I can use to set up a gibe preventer. I've done some research on the net."

"Now you're talking. With the way you sail, I'd say a gibe preventer is a must have."

"The block on the boom vang has seen better days too. I'll see what else I can fix as I go along."

"Do your worst. As long as I don't come back to the boat and find you've hung pink curtains in the cabin."

"We'd better get the sails down," Jon said thirty minutes later. "I'll start the engine."

They were approaching the entrance to the harbour.

"Not yet," Harriet insisted. "I hate that motor – it stinks."

"It is a bit old," Jon admitted. "Can we at least drop the foresail?"

"Chicken," Harriet uncleated the sheet and furled in the sail.

The boat started to slow down. "Let's sail her in."

"Are you mad? There's a twenty-knot blow on our rear end. We'll hit the jetty and rip a hole in the hull. Besides, if anybody sees us we'll be in trouble."

Harriet knew he was right. It was foolhardy to even think of sailing onto the jetty with such a strong wind blowing.

"You'd better get that old engine started then. I'll let the main flap a bit."

She waited until she heard the familiar chug-chug of the old diesel motor and loosened the main halyard. The sail slid halfway down the mast.

"Just in case the engine dies on us," she added.

* * *

They reached the marina and Harriet let the mainsail slip all the way down the mast. Jon motored up to the jetty and Harriet stepped off to secure the painters fore and aft. She tied the ropes around the bollards and hopped back aboard.

"I'll pack her up," she offered just as her phone started to ring in her pocket. She took it out and frowned. It was DI Jack Killian. Whenever Killian phoned her on her day off it never boded well. Harriet's day off was almost definitely going to be cancelled.

"Harriet," Killian said. "Where are you?"

"At the marina. We spent the night out on the water. We've just this minute got in."

"You went out in that gale? Is Jon Finch there with you?"

"Of course. What's wrong?"

"Gilly Landell found a body at the farm. The body of a young woman. It looks like she's had her head bashed in. I wouldn't bother you but DS Duncan's off with the flu and Eric White's still on leave."

"What about Thomas?"

"Manning the front desk at the station."

"Landell's Farm, you say?"

"That's right."

"I know where it is."

All thoughts of messing around on a boat suddenly drifted away.

"I'll be there in an hour," Harriet looked down at The Wandering Albatross and sighed. "We've just got to pack the boat up."

CHAPTER THREE

Landell's farm was a ten-minute drive inland from Trotterdown. Harriet rarely drove inland unless she really had to. She felt drawn by the sea and the rugged coastline. For Harriet, the harsh crags and weather-beaten cliffs were strangely tranquil. The landscape changed as she drove through flat farmland and reached Landell's Farm. She spotted Jack Killian's car and drove up to it. The red Ford Granada belonging to Alan Littlemore, the head of forensics, was parked further away in one of the fields.

DI Killian was talking to a man who looked to be roughly the same age as Harriet – William Landell Junior – she assumed. He was a short man with thick brown hair and a thin moustache.
"Morning, boss," Harriet said to Killian. "Morning." She looked at the young farmer.
"Harriet," Killian said. "This is William Landell Junior. William, this is DC Harriet Taylor."
"Gilly spotted the crows," Landell told her. "We've lost a few sheep to foxes in the past, so she thought that's what must have happened. She thought the birds were feeding on a dead sheep."
"Littlemore and his team are busy at the scene," Killian said. "And I'm sure Alan will appreciate it if we leave them in peace for a while."
"Gilly's in a bit of a state." William said. "She's in the house."
"William, I'm sure you both could use a strong cup of tea. I certainly could."

William led them towards an old stone farmhouse. Two large quad bikes were parked next to it. They appeared to have been modified for work on the farm – large steel frames had been welded onto the backs of them, probably for the purpose of transporting smaller livestock.

The farmhouse looked like it had seen better days. It was in dire need of repair. Chunks of stone had crumbled off the walls – the roof appeared to have been patched and re-patched many times and quite a few of the windows were broken.

"I'll get around to the repairs when I get time," William saw that Harriet was looking at the almost derelict building. "It didn't seem to bother my dad. I think he was so used to the way the place looked - he stopped seeing how bad it actually was. Come in, I'll put the kettle on."

Harriet and Killian followed him inside a huge kitchen. It wasn't what Harriet had expected. It wasn't at all what she pictured a farmhouse kitchen to look like. A huge granite-topped table stood in the centre of the room. The work areas were also topped with granite. The appliances all appeared to be modern.

"My Mum insisted," William seemed to have noticed the expression of surprise on Harriet's face. He switched on the kettle. "She agreed to the farm life, but she insisted there were to be some compromises. She loved to cook, you see. The first thing my dad had to do was get rid of the range and install a modern gas oven. That range had been here since my dad was a boy. Take a seat."

"Where's Gilly now?" Killian asked.

"She's having a lie down," William replied. "It's been quite a shock for her. She's six months pregnant."

"And yet she still works on the farm?" Harriet was shocked.

"You try and stop her. Gilly grew up on farms. Her Dad had a pig farm further down south near Grubton."

"What time did she discover the body?" Killian asked.

"It was around eight," William replied. "I'd just finished checking on the milking and Gilly was out scouting for rogue sheep. Some of them wander off during the night. That's why we bought the quad bikes – it makes it quicker to get around on the farm. She spotted a whole load of crows and rooks over by the outcrop of rocks on the far field. Like I said earlier, she assumed a fox had got hold of a sheep and the crows were finishing it off. The woman was lying there, hidden by the rocks. I went and had a look when Gilly came back and told me. She'd been covered with a load of branches, but the wind last night must have blown them away. We had quite a gale last night."

Harriet's thoughts drifted back to the night she'd spent at sea. The wind had howled all night long.

"Did you recognise the woman?" she asked. "Do you know who she could be?"

"Her face was a bit of a mess. One of her eyes was missing and the birds had done a good job on her, but I can't say I've seen her before."

"Have you noticed anything suspicious going on in the past day or so?" Killian asked him.

"What do you mean?"

"People hanging around. Strangers that don't have any business here?"

"No. We get the odd rambler coming through. It's a bit early in the season for them, but there are still a few brave ones who hike this time of year. The hiking path goes right past the rocks where the woman was lying. Dad never had a problem with hikers as long as they followed the rules – make sure they close the gates and don't worry the animals – that sort of thing."

"So, parts of the farm are open to the general public?" Harriet said.

"Always has been. The trail that runs through the farm is part of the three-day coast-to-coast hike. It starts in Grubton in the south and ends up in Trotterdown. It's a popular hike."
"How many people work here?"
"There are six of us altogether. Me, Gilly and two permanents plus two casuals I use during the busy times – the lambing for example."
"We'll need their names and contact details," Killian said.

There was a knock on the kitchen door and a very red-faced Alan Littlemore walked in.
"Morning," he nodded to Harriet. "Jack." He addressed Killian. "Can I have a word?"
"Excuse me," Killian stood up and followed the head of forensics outside.
"How long have you had the farm?" Harriet asked William.
"It's been in the family for the best part of a century. My dad was at the helm for thirty-five years. He passed away last year so now it's my responsibility."
"What do you farm?"
"Mostly sheep. We've got a few cows and pigs, but the sheep are by far the most cost-effective."

Killian came back inside.
"William, we'll need to talk to you again and we'll definitely need to talk to your wife. Let us know when she's up to it. We'll also need that list of everybody who works here, but for now we'll leave you to get on with your work."
And take care of your pregnant wife, Harriet thought but kept quiet.
"What will happen to the body?" William asked.
"Forensics have almost finished so she'll be taken away shortly. I'd appreciate if you didn't mention this to anybody just yet."

"I'm not one for gossip, nor is Gilly. We keep ourselves to ourselves."
"Good. It's going to get out sooner or later anyway, but it'll be better if we can work in peace until then. We'll be in touch."

"What's going on?" Harriet asked Killian outside. "I've seen that look on Littlemore's face before. Something's wrong isn't it."
"Follow me."
They walked across the field to the pile of rocks where the body had been found. Littlemore was bent over the rocks. He appeared to be digging away at something. The body had been covered with a plastic sheet.
Littlemore looked up. "She's not a pretty sight."
Harriet took a deep breath, removed the sheet and took it all in. The woman was dressed in a T-Shirt and jeans. Her arms were covered in scratches and bruises, as was her face. Dried blood had stuck her blonde hair to the side of her face and one of her eyes was missing."
"Any idea as to the cause of death?" Killian asked.
"I'd say it was a blow or two to the side of the head. The path guys will give us more, but I am pretty sure this is where she was killed. There's a lot of blood on the surrounding rocks."
"That's something, I suppose," Killian mused. "If she was killed here, at least we don't have to start looking around for other crime scenes."
"The path guys will give us time of death," Littlemore added. "But if I were to hazard a guess I'd say she's only been here a short while."
"Two or three days?" Harriet suggested.
"Maybe less. And it looks like the birds got away with one of her eyes."
"Did you find anything else?" Harriet asked. "Any kind of weapon?"
"We've bagged a few of the smaller rocks that could have been used to bash her over the head. We'll take them back with us."

"What about fragments of clothing? Anything else that shouldn't be here?"

"You could say that." He crouched down and pointed to a gap between the rocks. "One of my guys had a good look around and he found something in there that definitely shouldn't be there."

"What is it, Alan?" Killian said.

"Don't touch anything," he handed the DI a torch. "But have a look for yourself."

Killian did as he was told. He shone the torch inside the gap.

"Bloody hell. What's going on here?" He gave the torch to Harriet.

The gap was roughly three inches wide. Harriet shone the torch inside. There was an open area of around five square feet inside the rocks. She moved the torch and focused on something against the far rocks. It was a shape she couldn't quite make out at first, but it was definitely not part of the rock it was lying on. Two tattered brown boots were still attached to fleshless legs. Harriet shone the torch up the body and gasped when she saw what used to be a head. Thin wisps of black hair still sprouted from the grey skull.

CHAPTER FOUR

"You don't need to be an expert to know that poor bastard's been here a lot longer than her," Littlemore pointed to the young woman lying under the sheet. "A hell of a lot longer."

"Two bodies found in the same place," Harriet said. "What are the odds on that happening?"

"Astronomical," Killian said. "Something really odd is going on here."

"Do you think there's a connection?"

"Harriet how could there be. The woman's only been here for a few days at the most, whereas…" He gazed at the gap in the rocks. "Who knows how long he's been buried in there?"

"He?"

"I'm just speculating. From the size of the boots, I'd say it's a man."

"We're going to need some help," Littlemore said. "We'll need some lifting equipment and specialised tools."

"What for?" Harriet asked.

"We need to clear those rocks. They're much too heavy to lift. We're going to need access to our mystery man if we're going to be able to peel him off the rocks."

The thought made Harriet's stomach turn.

"The Fire Department should be able to help," Killian suggested. "I'll get onto it."

He took out his phone and walked away from the scene. Harriet had the urge to do the same. One body, she could cope with – it had become a part of her job, but this was something else altogether.

Killian returned a few minutes later.

"The Fire Department is on the way. They've been informed of what's required of them and they're bringing the necessary equipment. An ambulance will be here shortly, too. To take her away." He pointed to the body covered in the sheet. "Jon Finch is going to have his hands full with these two."

Harriet scanned the area around her. The farmhouse was roughly two hundred metres away across a field to the west. The path that formed part of the coast-to coast hike was about thirty metres away from the rocks.

"What are you thinking?" Killian asked her.

"There's nobody around," Harriet pointed out. "You can see the farm house from here, but behind it, the fields aren't really visible. There's also nobody using the path. We've been here a while and we haven't seen a single soul."

"What do you expect? It's Monday in early March. The tourist season won't start for at least another month."

"I think they came along the hiking trail – the woman and whoever killed her. If Littlemore's right and she was actually killed here, I mean."

"I'm inclined to take Littlemore's word for it."

"And I think she was killed during the day."

"The T-Shirt?"

"Exactly. The days have been warm but it's still chilly at night. I doubt anybody would come out here at night wearing just a T-Shirt."

"I'm going to extend the crime scene," the head of forensics had been listening in. "We'll cordon off the path fifty metres in each direction and I want the field out of bounds too. You'd better let farmer Brown know."

"Landell," Killian corrected him.

"What about the other body?" Harriet asked. "I think Landell Junior needs to know there's been a body hidden on his farm for who knows how long."

"This can't get out just yet," as usual, Killian was thinking about damage control. "Word will soon get out about the dead woman, but the other body needs to be kept quiet for the time being."

"I agree," Harriet knew exactly how the press would react. "Two bodies found in the same spot years apart will lead to all kinds of speculation. William Landell Junior also needs to be informed of the importance of discretion."

"I'll talk to him," Killian offered. "I've known the Landells a good few years. They're good people. I'll also get that list of employees from him. It's lambing time so they'll probably all be here helping out anyway. There's nothing more we can do here. The Fire Department will be along soon." He turned to Alan Littlemore. "How are you planning on scraping what's left of that poor bastard off the rocks?"

"I can be quite creative when I put my mind to it, Jack."

"Harriet," Killian said. "We'll start by talking to the employees. If the woman was here during the day, one of them might have seen something. Get hold of Eric and tell him his leave has been cut short and let Thomas know he's to find someone to relieve him at the front desk. We need to speak to everybody here and I need every experienced officer I can muster."

* * *

Donovan Beech was busy with the sheep. Killian and Harriet found him in one of the large paddocks. He was holding one of the ewes down, and he appeared to be cutting its hooves. He didn't even notice the two detectives watching him. He finished with the ewe, released her and she ran to join her friends in the corner.

"Donovan Beech?" Killian said.

Beech looked up. He was a broad-shouldered man in his early fifties. He had a ruddy complexion and a bulbous nose that suggested he liked a drink or two after work. His black hair was turning grey in places.

"What do you want?" he asked.

"Can we have a word?" Killian said.

"We can talk while I work. I've got over a hundred ewes to trim before the days out. If that's alright with you?"

Without waiting for an answer, he opened the gate of the adjoining paddock, grabbed hold of another sheep and dragged her, rather violently into the space where he was working."

"What are you doing?" Harriet asked him. "I'm DC Taylor and this is DI Killian. We're from the Trotterdown police."

"I know who you are. I'm trimming the ewes. What does it look like I'm doing? We don't want them getting foot rot, do we?"

Friendly chap, Harriet thought.

Donovan Beech carried on trimming.

"Mr Beech," Killian said. "We need to talk to you whether you like it or not."

"Talk away," Beech finished with the ewe and yanked another one away from the safety of its friends.

"A young woman was found dead over by the footpath this morning." This information didn't seem to have any effect on the ruddy-faced farmhand.

"We're treating the death as suspicious," Killian continued. "And we need to ask you if you've noticed anything unusual going on here over the last few days."

"Unusual?" he looked up at Killian and in doing so he loosened his grip on a particularly feisty ewe. The sheep let rip, and Beech took the full force of one of her hooves on the chin.

Harriet started to giggle – she couldn't help herself.

"You little bugger," Beech rubbed his chin. "What do you mean by unusual?"

"People hanging around who shouldn't be here?" Killian explained. "We have good reason to believe she was here during the day. Did you notice anybody hanging around here?"

"By the hiking trail you say?" he rubbed his chin harder - the ewe had given him quite a kick. "I can't say I did. I've been working mostly down here. It's lambing season in case you didn't know. It's the busiest time of the year. The ewes have to be vaccinated and we have to keep a close eye on them. It's a twenty-four-hour job – all hands on deck if you know what I mean. Anyway, you can't really see the trail from here."

He was right. The farmhouse was in the way.

"How long have you been working here?" Harriet asked him.

"Pretty much all my life. I was born in one of the fields if you must know. 1968. The summer of love or thereabouts. My folks were hippy types. Old man Landell didn't have a problem with them camping out as long as they helped out when it was busy. Peace, happiness and love and all that kind of crap. Where do you think I got this ridiculous name from?"

"Donovan?"

"He was supposed to be some kind of Scottish Bob Dylan. You're Scottish - you must know who Donovan is. Can I get back to work now?"

"Of course," Killian said. "If you think of anything else, please give me a call."

He took out one of his cards and held it out. Beech looked at it as if it were a dog turd.

"If I think of anything else, I know where to get hold of you." He finished clipping the ewe and opened the gate to make a start on another one.

CHAPTER FIVE

"Well, he was a pleasure to talk to," Harriet said to Killian by the DI's car. "I'm glad that sheep kicked him in the face."
"Farmers. He's old school. They think we should be eternally grateful to them for putting food on our table. They're not all like that – Landell Junior's old man was a real gentleman."
The two PC's White arrived in Thomas's car. Harriet could see straight away that Eric wasn't happy about having his leave cut short. He was pouting like a five-year-old.
"I'm sorry about this, Eric," Killian said to him. "It couldn't be helped. Duncan is off sick, and we need everybody we can spare on this one."
"Hungover, more like it," Eric scoffed. "I've lost count of how many times the DS has phoned in sick on a Monday."
   Killian filled the Whites in on what had happened.
"Two bodies?" Thomas exclaimed when the DI had finished.
"That's right. But it's the woman we're going to concentrate on for the time being. The other one's going to be a bit tricky. God knows how long he's been here. It's lambing season so all the farm workers will be here. That should make our job easier. All the employees, temps included will be on the farm. We have reason to believe the woman was killed where she was found, and we also think she was killed during the day. She was only wearing a T-Shirt and a pair of jeans."
"It was bloody freezing last night," Eric White pointed out.
"Tell me about it," Harriet said. "I spent the night out on a boat."
"You and Jon Finch are getting quite cosy, aren't you?" Thomas said.
"I can hear wedding bells in the air," Eric added. "And then a honeymoon to the catacombs of France."

"That's enough, you two," Killian said. "Littlemore has finished at the scene. Both bodies have been taken away. We need to talk to everybody who has been working on the farm for the past few days."

* * *

Two hours later they were finished. None of the farm workers remembered seeing anything odd by the rocks or on the hiking trail. Most of the farm hands had been helping out with the sheep – it was the busiest time of the year and all their efforts had been spent on the lambs that were being born.

"What now, boss?" Harriet asked.

The appearance of a woman in her early thirties answered Harriet's question. The pregnant woman was obviously William Landell Junior's wife, Gilly.

"Mrs Landell," Killian said. "How are you feeling?"

"I've been better. William said you'd want to speak to me."

"I'm afraid so. Shall we go inside?"

"I'd rather talk out here if that's alright with you. I need some fresh air."

"When's the baby due?" Harriet asked her.

"Middle of June. A summer baby. We didn't plan it that way but I'm glad."

"Could you talk us through what happened this morning?" Killian said.

"I'd had a bad night – this little bugger keeps me awake with his kicking sometimes," she patted her belly. "So, I was up before William. By the time he got up I'd already checked on the sheep and made sure they were all alright. At around eight, I was in the field by the pond when I spotted a load of birds over by the rocks next to the coast-to-coast trail. I feared the worst."

"Foxes?" Harriet suggested.

"We've lost a few sheep to them in the past few weeks. I jumped on one of the quads and went to take a look. Since William got the quads it's been a lot easier to get around the farm. The frames on the back are big enough to carry a sheep if we need to. The woman was just lying there. The birds had already done quite a job on her."

Harriet noticed that Gilly Landell appeared very calm under the circumstances.

"Did you recognise the woman?" she asked.

"Never seen her before."

"Are you going to be alright?"

"I was born on a farm. My Dad had the place on the way to Grubton. Farm life toughens you up a bit. Death comes with the territory."

"Thank you, Mrs Landell," Killian said. "I wish you all the best with the baby."

"It's a boy," she told him. "Another Landell to take over the farm one day."

"Where do we go from here?" Harriet asked Killian when Gilly Landell had gone back inside the farmhouse.

"Unfortunately for us, the scene of the crime is hidden from where all of the action on the farm has taken place over the past few days. Our next step is to find out who the dead woman is. Littlemore didn't find any ID on her, but somebody must be missing her by now."

"I was on duty all weekend," Thomas said. "Nobody's filed a missing person report."

"Somebody must know who this woman is. William Landell didn't recognise her, nor did his wife, me, Harriet or Littlemore. That suggests she's not local. We need to check all the guesthouses, B&B's and hotels in the area."

"And the Backpackers," Harriet suggested. "She was young. She could've been staying at the Backpackers in Trotterdown."

"We'll cover them all while we wait and see what Littlemore and his team can tell us. Dr Finch ought to have a time of death for us before the end of the day, too."

Thomas White nudged Harriet in the ribs.

"Thomas," Killian said. "Stop behaving like a ten-year-old and start acting like a policeman."

"Is the Doc going to have to examine the other body?" Eric White asked. "The one that's been hidden here for years?"

"I expect so," Killian replied. "But, like I said, that's not our main priority at the moment. Once we have a definite TOD on the woman we'll be able to narrow things down a bit."

* * *

The Backpackers in Trotterdown was situated two streets away from the harbour. During the summer months it was always packed to the brim but in early March, Harriet expected it to be quiet. She and Killian walked through the archway and stopped at the reception desk. A man with long brown hair was so engrossed in something on his tablet, he didn't even realise they were standing there.

"Excuse me," Killian said.

The man looked up at them.

"Sorry, "he said. "I was miles away there."

He cast them a puzzled look. Harriet and Killian didn't look like two people who were looking for a room at a backpackers.

"DI Killian," Killian showed him his ID. "And this is DC Taylor. We're from the Trotterdown Police. Can we have a word?"

"Of course. The name's Ian, Ian Swift."

"Mr Swift, we're trying to establish the identity of a young woman. Early twenties, blonde hair. Do you have anybody matching that description staying here?"

"The place is pretty dead at the moment. We have a couple of Aussies, some Americans and a Canadian. And there's the French couple. Lauren has blonde hair."

"Are the French couple here now?"

"I think so. They came last Friday. They booked for a week. They're probably in the Courtyard. The bar's closed now but they sometimes sit there and read."

He led them down a carpeted corridor to a kind of indoor garden. Tables and chairs were set out in the centre. A small bar stood against the wall in the corner. A thin, tanned man was sitting at one of the tables reading a book. He was smoking a particularly pungent smelling cigarette.

"Jean," Ian said. "These people would like a word. They're from the police. And you know you're not allowed to smoke in here."

Jean looked up from his book and breathed a cloud of smoke in Harriet's direction.

"How can I help you?" he spoke directly to her.

He spoke English with a slight American accent.

"We're looking for a young woman," Killian said.

"Me too," Jean stubbed his cigarette out on a saucer. "Do you know where I can find one?"

Harriet took an instant dislike to the man.

He thinks he's a gigolo, she thought.

"Excuse et moi," he held out his hand to her. "Jean Dupont. I'm from Paris."

Harriet ignored the hand.

"I believe you're here with a woman?" she said.

"Lauren, that's right."

"Where's Lauren now?"

"She should be in Grubton by now."

"Grubton?"

"It's the start of the coast-to-coast trail. Lauren is doing the hike backwards. Where do you get your town names from? Grubton? It's hardly an appetising name is it?"

"Are you saying that Lauren is doing the coast-to-coast?" Killian asked him.

"That's right. You English and your hiking. How do you call it? Rambling?"

"And you didn't go with her?" Harriet said.

"Of course not. I didn't come here to ramble."

"What *did* you come here for?" Harriet didn't know why but she had a sudden urge to knock the smug smile from this arrogant Frenchman's face.

"I like to get away from Paris in the springtime," he smiled as though he'd made a huge joke.

"When did Lauren set off?" Killian asked.

"Saturday morning. Early. I was still in bed when she left. We do our own thing. That's the kind of relationship we have if you know what I mean."

He grinned at Harriet. It was a grin that made her stomach turn.

"Do you have a photograph of Lauren?" Killian asked.

"Of course," Jean took out his phone and opened up his photo files.

"That's her there. That was in Edinburgh for New Year."

The photograph showed a pretty blonde woman. A pretty blonde woman who was now lying on a table in the mortuary a few miles away.

CHAPTER SIX

Doctor Jon Finch opened the door for Jean Dupont and placed a hand on his shoulder.

"I'm sorry."

Jean's face had lost most of its colour, and the arrogant smile was long gone. He'd just identified the woman lying on the table in the mortuary as his girlfriend, Lauren. Lauren Moreau was twenty-two years old. She was a student in her final year of University.

"There's some paperwork that needs to be filled in," Finch told him. "And the police will need to talk to you again. I'm sure you'll want to get hold of Lauren's family, too."

"Her parents are both dead. She has a brother, but they haven't spoken to each other in years. I'm the only family she really had. I still can't believe she's dead."

Dr Finch looked at his face and he believed him. He seemed genuinely shocked.

Harriet and Killian walked down the corridor towards them. Harriet knew immediately that the dead woman was Jean Dupont's girlfriend. The expression on the Frenchman's face told it all.

"We need to talk to you down at the station," Killian informed him.

"I can't believe she's dead. We were planning on heading up to Wales after this."

"There are a few forms that Mr Dupont needs to fill in," Finch said.

"Then he's all yours."

"Can we have a word?" Killian asked the lanky pathologist.

"Of course," Finch said and smiled at Harriet. "Come through to my office."

They sat down at Finch's desk.

"What have you got for us?" Killian asked.

"Cause of death was a couple of blows to the side of the head. Something heavy was used – possibly a rock. We didn't find any indication of sexual assault. She died around noon yesterday, give or take an hour or two."

"She was killed during the day?" Harriet asked.

"That's right."

"Then somebody might have seen something," Killian said. "The part of the path that runs past the Landell's farm is about five miles from Trotterdown. Somebody must have seen her."

"There's one thing I don't understand," Harriet said.

"Go on."

"The woman's boyfriend told us she left the Backpackers early on Saturday. If she was killed around noon on Sunday, it means she'd only covered five miles in over twenty-four hours. It doesn't make any sense."

"We'll be sure to ask the boyfriend about it," Killian said.

"What about the other one," Harriet said. "Have you had a chance to have a look at the other body?"

"That one's going to take some more time," Finch said. "I don't expect we'll get an accurate time of death from him."

"So, it is a man then?" Killian said.

"Definitely. I'll have a better idea of what happened to him by the end of the day but, like I said, I'm not expecting to find out much. I can tell you this, though, I examined something similar when I was still a student – the body of a woman who'd been dead for fifteen years and this one's very similar. The decomposition, I mean."

"Fifteen years?" Harriet said.

"There's no rush," Killian said. "I don't think we'll be able to do much about that one."
Harriet was shocked. She couldn't believe the DI was just going to push the discovery of a body under the carpet.
"Aren't you even curious?" she asked him.
"He's been dead for years, Harriet. All the evidence will probably have been eaten away by now. Besides, we have more pressing matters to attend to. The death of the French woman is our main priority at the moment. I'm sure the Super will agree with me. We have a dead French woman whose boyfriend needs to be interviewed."

* * *

An hour later, Jean Dupont sat opposite Killian and Harriet in one of the interview rooms at Trotterdown police station.
"Mr Dupont," Killian began. "I know this is hard – we're very sorry about your girlfriend, but it has to be done, I'm afraid. When did you last see Lauren?"
"Saturday morning," Dupont said. "I've already told you that."
"How did she seem?" Harriet asked.
"What do you mean, how did she seem?"
"Exactly that. How was Lauren? Was she acting strange in any way?"
"No. She was the same as always. She was excited about doing the coast-to-coast."
"And you didn't go with her?" Killian said.
"I told you that, too. I don't do rambling."
"So Lauren set off on Saturday morning," Harriet said. "What time was it, exactly?"
"Around seven. It's a fifty-kilometre walk, a two-day hike. I've told you that already, too. Why do I have to keep repeating myself?"

Lauren left at seven on Saturday morning, Harriet thought. *Dr Finch put the time of death at around noon on Sunday.*
"There's something I don't understand," she said. "If Lauren left at seven on Saturday, isn't it a bit odd that she'd only covered a few miles by Sunday afternoon?"
Jean Dupont seemed to get the gist of what Harriet was implying. His eyebrows creased as though he was thinking hard.
"Yes, it is odd," he agreed eventually. "Lauren liked to walk quickly. She should have been halfway to Grubton by then."
"Where were you yesterday?" Killian couldn't put off the question any longer.
"At the Backpackers, I suppose."
"You suppose?"
"I was there. I got up at around ten and spent most of the day lounging around in the courtyard. I read the Sunday papers."
"Can anybody corroborate this?"
"Why are you asking me this? Do you think I had something to do with Lauren's death?"
"We have to ask you. Is there anybody who can confirm you were at the Backpackers yesterday?"
"Ian was working behind the bar. He'll be able to confirm it."
"We'll be sure to check."
"Your English is very good," Harriet commented.
"I spent four years in Ohio. I went to the University there."
"Let's go back to the timeline," Killian said. "You said that Lauren left the Backpackers at seven, and you said she walked quite quickly. The few miles to Landell's farm should've only taken her a couple of hours. It's flat terrain most of the way. Somewhere along the path she was obviously distracted in some way. Can you explain that?"

"No, I can't. Why are you asking me all these things?"
"Was she maybe planning on meeting up with anybody?" Harriet suggested.
"No, she was doing the hike on her own."
"What was Lauren wearing when she set off?"
"Jeans, a T-Shirt and a sweater. It was still a bit chilly when she left."
"And she was planning on spending the night somewhere around the halfway point?"
"There's a guesthouse in Crayford. It's almost exactly halfway."
"I know where it is," Killian said.
"She'd booked to spend Saturday night there."
"But she never made it further than Landell's farm."
"Did she have a backpack with her?" Harriet remembered they hadn't found anything at the scene.
"She took a small rucksack. She keeps some spare clothes in there. A rain coat and some toiletries."

"Thank you, Mr Dupont," Killian turned off the recording device. "We'll need to check with the barman at the Backpackers, and we'll take it from there. I expect you'll be going back to France now?"
"No. I think I'll stick to the itinerary. In Lauren's memory, if you like. There's nothing for me in France."
"How long will you be staying at the Backpackers?" Harriet asked him.
"Until Friday. We paid in advance, so I might as well stick around."
"We may need to speak with you again," Killian told him.
"I've got nothing to hide," he stood up and left the room.

CHAPTER SEVEN

"What did you make of him?" Killian asked Harriet in the canteen. She was sipping a cup of black tea.
"He's a hard one to figure out. He seemed genuinely shocked about Lauren's death."
"How many times have you seen *genuinely shocked*, Harriet?"
"I know – he could be faking it, but I really can't picture him as a killer. He's full of himself but I don't think he killed his girlfriend."
"We'll see."
"What now?"
"Seeing as though Duncan is man down, there's just the four of us. Thomas and I are the oldest, so we'll take the Backpackers. I want to find out more about Lauren Moreau and check out her boyfriend's alibi. I also want to ask around to see if anybody saw Lauren Moreau on Saturday or Sunday."
"What about me and Eric?"
"Put your hiking boots on. I want the two of you to walk from the Backpackers to Landell's farm. See if you can find anything along the way to give us a clue to what happened to that poor woman. If you're quick, you can be back before it gets dark."

* * *

"This isn't why I joined the police," PC Eric White griped. "To go trudging around the bloody countryside. I hate hiking – never seen the point of it."
Harriet and Eric had started out from Trotterdown and were making their way towards Landell's farm. The coast-to-coast road was well maintained. There were wooden benches placed every half a mile or so for the hikers to take a breather.

"Come on, Eric," Harriet picked up the pace a bit. "Enjoy the scenery. It's beautiful around here."

"Beautiful, my arse. I'm definitely too young for this place. Time to move to the big city I think."

They continued on for a short while. Eric was very red in the face – he was obviously not used to walking so far.

"What exactly are we looking for?" he asked.

"Anything to suggest the French woman was here. Her boyfriend told us she had a small rucksack with her. We didn't find it where her body was found."

"What do you think happened to her?"

"I have no idea. Somewhere between where we are now and Landell's farm, she was murdered. We don't know if she met someone along the way or if she was followed and attacked."

"What about her boyfriend?"

"He's in the clear. His alibi at the Backpackers checked out. I didn't think it was him anyway."

A woman appeared on the path in the distance. As she got closer, Harriet saw she was walking a young-looking Spaniel. The dog barked at Eric as they passed. The woman stared at Eric's uniform.

"Excuse me," Harriet said to her. "Do you walk your dog along here often?"

"Every day. In the winter and spring, anyway."

"Sorry," Harriet took out her ID and showed it to her. "DC Taylor. We're trying to find out if a young woman came this way on Saturday or Sunday. Blonde, around my height."

"There was someone like that here on Saturday morning."

The dog jumped up at Eric and started chewing one of the buttons on his uniform.

"Sorry," the woman said. "He still needs a bit of training."
"He's a Spaniel, isn't he?" Eric asked. "We used to have one when I was a kid. They never stop. Ours was like a whirlwind."
"The blonde woman," Harriet said. "What time did you see her on Saturday?"
"It was around eight, I suppose."
"Where was she?"
"Almost exactly where we are now. I walk a mile along the path and a mile back every day. I turn around when I get to the second bench."
Eight in the morning, Harriet thought. *That would make sense if Lauren had set off at seven.*
"What was she wearing?" she asked.
"Jeans, T-Shirt and a pair of hiking boots. She was miles away."
"What do you mean?"
"She seemed lost in her own world. And she walked quickly like she was walking with a purpose."
"Did you notice anybody else around that morning?"
"No. It was nice and quiet. It always is this time of the year. In a couple of months, this path will be like the M1. What's this all about anyway?"
"Just a routine enquiry," Harriet gave her the standard reply. "Thank you. Enjoy the rest of your walk."

"So, she was here at eight on Saturday morning," Harriet said to Eric. "What happened to her between then and noon on Sunday?"
"It's a mystery. My feet are bloody killing me. These shoes weren't designed for paths like this."
"Stop whining, Eric. I reckon it'll take us another hour or so to walk to where Lauren Moreau's body was dumped. Why did it take her over a day to walk it? Unless…"

She took out her phone and dialled Dr Finch's number.

"Jon," she said. "I need to ask you something."

"I'm knackered," Finch said. "That's if you were going to ask me out again. I'm looking forward to an early night tonight."

"I wasn't, no. We've had a confirmed sighting of someone who could be our French woman. She was seen on the path a few miles from Landell's farm. She was seen at eight on Saturday morning. You put the time of death at around noon on Sunday."

"Give or take an hour or two, that's right."

"Is there any way you can tell if her body was dumped while she was still alive?"

"What are you suggesting?"

"I think she was attacked on Saturday," Harriet explained. "I think the killer thought she was dead and dumped her body at the far edge of Landell's farm, but she was actually still alive. She was covered in branches and left by the rocks."

"I'll have to do another examination," Finch told her. "If you're right and she was still alive when she was covered up there may be traces of the branches in her mouth and throat. She might have breathed in small bits of bark. I can tell you that the scratches on her face and arms were made before she died. That could tie in with your theory – they may have been caused by the branches being placed on top of her. I'll let you know what I find out later today. The other corpse will have to wait though."

"That's fine. Killian doesn't seem to think we'll get much out of that one anyway."

She rang off.

"Does he get a sore neck when he kisses you?" Eric asked. "Or does he make you stand on a beer crate?"

"Shut up, Eric. If I'm right about this, it means that Lauren Moreau was covered with branches while she was still alive. She lay there for over twenty-four hours before she died."
"It also means our Frenchman's alibi for yesterday is irrelevant."
"What a horrible way to die," Harriet tried to picture what had happened. "She was attacked with a rock or something similar and left for dead. She was only wearing a T-Shirt and a pair of jeans. It must have been freezing out here all night. The blows to her head got her in the end but it must have been awful lying there, not being able to find help."

They carried on walking. On their right the fields that formed part of Landell's Farm spread out. Sheep were grazing on the grass. The smoke coming out of the farmhouse in the distance was clearly visible from the path. They were about a mile away from Landell's farm when Harriet spotted something. It was something black – partially hidden in a cluster of bushes about five metres away from the path. She took a closer look. She moved the bushes to one side and smiled.
"It looks like we've found Lauren Moreau's rucksack."

CHAPTER EIGHT

Alan Littlemore arrived forty-five minutes later. The closest road to that particular spot on the path was the one that led to Landell's farm and the head of forensics was sweating profusely by the time he got there.
"I need to get more exercise," he panted. "What's the urgency?"
"Where's the rest of your team?" Harriet asked him.
"Back at the lab. What have we got?"
"I think that's the dead girl's rucksack," Harriet pointed to the black bag in the bushes. "It has to be hers."

Littlemore got to work. He put on a pair of gloves and walked up to the bushes. He picked up the rucksack and placed it on the path.
"Let's have a look, shall we?" he opened up the zip and removed a red raincoat.
He then pulled out a waterproof bag that looked like it contained travel documents. He took out a passport.
"It's hers. Lauren Moreau. Twenty-two years old. Pretty girl. What on earth is the rucksack doing here? She was killed over a mile away. I know I've just walked it."
"I have a theory about that," Harriet told him what she suspected.
"So, you reckon she was still alive when she was covered in the branches?" Littlemore said when she'd finished.
"It looks like it. Dr Finch is busy examining her again but that's what I think happened."
"You could be right, but it still doesn't explain what her rucksack is doing over a mile away from where we found her."
"I've been thinking about that," Eric chipped in.

He'd removed his shoes and he was rubbing his feet. He was wearing odd socks.

"Go on," Littlemore urged.

"I think she ran."

"Ran?"

"I think she ran to try and get away from whoever was about to attack her. She could have dumped her pack, so she could run faster."

"Hmm," Littlemore sighed. "But she didn't run fast enough, did she?"

He scanned the area around them. On their left was wild vegetation – it hadn't been cleared for farming yet, and on their right was open farmland. The buildings of Landell's farm were clearly visible in the distance.

"She ran towards the farm," Harriet suggested. "I think she thought that if she could reach the farm, she'd be safe."

"But obviously whoever was chasing her was a better runner than she was," Littlemore said.

Harriet thought about Jean Dupont, Lauren's boyfriend. His alibi for yesterday was now worthless.

Could the chain-smoking Frenchman have been able to outrun his girlfriend?

She didn't think so. He was hardly the sporty type and Lauren was reasonably fit by all accounts.

Littlemore crouched down. He'd obviously spotted something on the path.

"Look at this. I think you could be right, Eric." He took a camera out of his bag and took a number of photographs in quick succession.

"There's definitely indentations on the path here and over there." He pointed to a spot about fifty centimetres away. "If I were to hazard a guess, I'd say a struggle took place right here. Look at how the dirt on

the path has been ripped up. She could have been attacked, broke free and tried to make a run for it."
"I should be a detective," Eric beamed from ear to ear.
"You've got a long way to go. And would you please put your shoes back on? Those odd socks make you look ridiculous."

Harriet, Eric and the head of forensics walked slowly towards Landell's farm. Littlemore carried Lauren Moreau's rucksack in a large plastic evidence bag.
"I'll get my guys to give this a once over when we get back to the lab, but I don't think we'll find much."
"Can we get a lift back with you?" Eric asked him. "I've got blisters on blisters down there." He pointed to his feet.
"I suppose so. I just want to have another look at where the body was found."

They walked the part of the path that ran through the farm and Littlemore stopped by the rocks where the two bodies had been found that morning.
"I'm still inclined to believe she was killed right here," Littlemore pointed to the rocks. "There's a lot of blood spatters on the rocks. My guys are going through the photos we took earlier but to me it looks like she was bashed on the head here and dragged down to the other rocks where she wouldn't be seen from the path or the farm."
"Maybe this is where he caught her up," Eric suggested. "She was heading for the safety of the farm, but she never made it that far."
"I think you're right again. He caught up with her, hit her with a rock and covered up the body."
"But she wasn't dead," Harriet reminded him.
"No, she wasn't. But he didn't know that, did he?"

"The woman walking the dog saw her a mile from Trotterdown at eight on Saturday morning. She can't remember seeing anybody else on the path that morning, so I'm inclined to think the killer came from the direction of the farm."
"Then Lauren would've walked straight into him," Eric pointed out.
"So what? Why would she even worry? She probably thought he was a hiker. She wouldn't have suspected a thing."
"He could have walked straight past her, turned around and attacked her," Littlemore added. "You two make quite a double act. Eric, if it weren't for those ridiculous socks, I'd have to admit you've gained a bit more respect from me today."
"Thanks," Eric said. "I think."

"Where to?" Littlemore asked as he drove away from Landell's farm and headed back to Trotterdown.
"Can you drop us at the station?" Harriet asked. "Killian wants us back for a briefing. Hopefully Dr Finch has found something from the second examination."
They drove in silence for a while. Harriet was glad when the blue of the Atlantic appeared in the distance. She didn't know why but the ocean always seemed to welcome her back, even when she'd only been away for a short while. She wondered when she would get another chance to go out on Jon Finch's boat. She had a feeling she was going to have to put it on hold for quite a while.

"Thanks," Harriet said to Littlemore outside the station.
The head of forensics drove away without saying a word.
"What do you make of him?" Eric asked. "I can't quite figure him out. Sometimes he's friendly and other times he's downright rude."
"He's a forensics expert. He has an analytical brain and I don't think social interaction is his forte."

"I hope the DI has something for us," Eric opened the door for Harriet and followed her inside the station.

* * *

Killian, Thomas White and a very red-nosed DS Duncan were waiting for them in the DI's office. Duncan sneezed as they came in and blew his nose with a handkerchief.

"I've just finished filling DS Duncan in on what's happened so far," Killian said. "Take a seat. I've just this minute got the report through from Dr Finch. It appears you were right, Harriet. The French woman had traces of dust and what Finch assumes are particles of the branches in her mouth and throat. The bruises on her back also suggest she was alive for quite some time after she was covered up."

"A woman walking her dog claims she saw Lauren at around eight on Saturday morning," Harriet told him. "And Littlemore found evidence of a struggle on the path near to where we found her rucksack. We think she was chased for over a mile and then killed."

"Chased?"

"She was probably attacked on the path, she broke free, and the killer chased her to the edge of the farm. He caught up with her and killed her right there."

"Frenchie's alibi for Sunday is irrelevant now," Eric reminded them.

"I realise that, Eric," Killian said.

"I still don't think he's the one," Harriet said. "You've met him, boss – can you imagine him having the stamina to chase someone for over a mile and then still have enough strength left in him to kill someone?"

"No, I can't," Killian admitted. "He chain-smokes those Camel things of his at an alarming rate. We'll need to speak to him again, anyway. What about the dog walker? Did she see anybody else on the path that day? Was there anyone else lurking around?"

"She didn't see anybody else. Only Lauren but I think our killer came from the opposite direction. The woman with the dog only walked a mile from Trotterdown. Lauren Moreau was chased a few miles away towards the Landell's farm."

"Do we have anything else?" Killian asked."

"What about the other body?" Harriet said. "Surely we're not going to ignore the other one."

"What other body?" this was clearly news to DS Duncan. He was suddenly interested.

"There was another body buried in the rocks not far from where the woman was found," Killian told him.

"In the rocks?" Duncan's eyes widened.

"And he's been there a lot longer than the French woman," Harriet added. "At least fifteen years longer."

Duncan looked like he was going to pass out. His face seemed to lose all of its colour. Even his red nose had turned pale.

"Are you alright?" Killian asked him.

"I don't feel too well," the DS stood up, and for a moment Harriet was afraid he was going to collapse. He teetered from side to side. "I think I'd better go home, Jack. I really don't feel well at all."

CHAPTER NINE

"What's wrong with him?" Eric White asked when Duncan had stumbled out of the room. "He looked like he was about to faint."

"Flu," Killian said.

"That looked worse than flu. He looked like someone had just walked over his grave. That was really creepy."

"Eric, let's press on, shall we? Thomas and I spoke to everyone staying in the Backpackers. They're all shocked as you can well imagine. The two Americans are even planning on leaving because of it. They don't feel safe. In Trotterdown of all places."

"Yanks," Eric scoffed. "Bunch of drama queens."

"Eric, since when did this xenophobia of yours start?"

"Xeno what?"

"Let's put your prejudices aside, shall we? And concentrate on the matter in hand. Like I said, we spoke to the other backpackers and none of them could tell us much. I'm inclined to agree with Harriet. I don't think Jean Dupont has the stamina to give chase for fifty metres, let alone over a mile. We'll speak to him again, of course, but my gut says we need to look elsewhere."

"Do you think the DS will be alright?" Thomas asked. "He really didn't look too hot back there."

"I feel terrible," Killian said. "I really thought he was milking it to get a few days off work. He really looked ill. I'm sure he'll be back to normal after a day or two of rest."

"What now then?" Eric asked.

"It's getting late. Go home and get some sleep. Tomorrow, I want to do a full sweep of that farm. Lambing season or not I want to pick the brains of everybody who was there over the weekend. Our killer was there, and I want to shake them up a bit – maybe we can refresh a few memories. I'm going to have a quick chat with Tanya, the press officer, then I'll be off home too. This is going to get out sooner or later – I just don't want the news of the second body to be common knowledge just yet."

"Damage control," the two Whites and Harriet said in unison.

"Am I that predictable? Anyway, the general public has a right to know about the French woman but a body that's remained hidden for over fifteen years? That's going to cause speculation and we can really do without that at the moment."

"We are going to investigate it though, aren't we?" Harriet said.

"Why are you so obsessed with a man who died when you were probably still in primary school?"

"I'm just curious. Don't you want to know how he got there?"

"Of course. But right now, we have a much more recent murder to focus on. Go home. We'll all meet at Landell's farm tomorrow at eight."

As Harriet drove home, her thoughts turned to DS Duncan's episode in Killian's office. Something about the body found in the rocks had disturbed him deeply.

That wasn't a symptom of the flu, she thought as she turned into her street and parked outside her house, *that was something else altogether.*

Duncan had acted like he was in shock.

* * *

Harriet went inside the house and made some tea. She took out her phone and called Dr Finch.

"Harriet," he sounded tired. "What can I do for the best-looking DC in Trotterdown?"

"I'm the only DC in Trotterdown, you fool. Are you still at work?"
"I was just about to finish up. I'm looking forward to a bath and then bed. What can I do for you?"
"Can you do me a favour?"
"Of course."
"Could you send over the reports from the two autopsies on the French girl?"
"Killian already has them."
"I know. I'm not at work. I've just got home. Could you email them to my home email address?"
"Don't you ever stop working?"
"No. Besides, what else am I supposed to do this evening? My boyfriend made it absolutely clear he wants to be on his own tonight, remember?"
"Boyfriend? I like the sound of that. In that case, how can I refuse? I'll mail them through to you now. Anything else?"
Harriet could tell he was yawning on the other end of the line.
"The other body," she said. "What do you think you'll be able to tell from it?"
"Not much, I'm afraid. Most of him will have been eaten away over time. Why are you so obsessed with an ancient corpse anyway?"
"Not you, too?"
"Sorry?"
"Nothing. I forgot to thank you for such a great time on the boat. I'm itching to go out again."
"We will. I promise."
"Good night, Jon. Sweet dreams."

Finch's reports came through five minutes later. Harriet read the second one first. Lauren Moreau was five feet eight tall and weighed eight stones. Her physical appearance was described as athletic. *Whoever chased her must have been very fit,* Harriet thought.
Dr Finch continued to state that she'd suffered extensive bruising on her back. The bruises were sustained before she died.
She was placed on her back and left for dead.

Harriet scrolled down. The report noted that she'd suffered severe haemorrhaging to her head. Three separate trauma sites were found. *She was hit three times with the rock.*
Finch went on to describe what he'd found in her nose, mouth and throat. Particles of the branches that were placed on top of her had been inhaled.
She was still breathing when the branches were used to cover her up.

Harriet then concentrated on the initial autopsy report. She already knew most of what it contained but she wanted to see if anything else jumped out at her. Cause of death was due to the haemorrhaging caused by the blows to the head. The time of death according to the body temperature, rigor and liver mortis was put at between noon and 2pm on Sunday.
She lay under those branches for roughly 27 hours, Harriet thought, and a cold shiver rushed through her body. The report didn't mention whether she'd been unconscious the whole time, or if she was actually aware of what was happening to her. Harriet hoped that she'd been out of it the whole time.

She made another cup of tea and read the first report again. There was no indication of sexual abuse.
Why was she killed?

Harriet knew that once sexual abuse had been ruled out in the case of the murder of a young, pretty woman, the motive became much trickier to establish. Her fingernails had been bitten short and there were no traces of human blood or skin under them.

Harriet closed her eyes and tried to picture what could have happened.

Lauren Moreau is a mile out from Trotterdown when she walks past a woman walking a dog. It's eight in the morning. Roughly three miles further along the path, she's attacked by somebody. Maybe he grabbed her rucksack. Maybe it was the killer who threw it in the bushes to cover his tracks. Lauren manages to break free and makes a run for it. She can see the farm in the distance, and she figures she'll be safe there. Her attacker still pursues her. A mile further down the path, he manages to catch her and knocks her out with a rock. He then buries her under a pile of branches and leaves. He doesn't know she's still alive.

Harriet opened her eyes.

"Why," she said out loud. "Why, why, why?"

Killian had always drummed it into her that motive was the key to any murder investigation and Harriet completely agreed with him. In ninety percent of cases it was the motive that gave the culprit away in the end.

There is no apparent motive for this murder.

She closed the computer down and finished her tea. She needed to sleep, but there were too many thoughts in her head.

Why would somebody want to kill a young French woman?

Why did DS Duncan react so strangely to the news of the body found in the rocks?

She went upstairs and lay down on the bed. She needed to sleep but too many things were rushing through her mind. She opened the drawer on the bedside table. The pill box was still there, and it was full. She took two of the blue capsules out and put them in her mouth. Harriet knew that, in twenty minutes or so they would turn the thoughts in her head into mist, and a dreamless sleep would follow.

CHAPTER TEN

1996

The door to the farmhouse was opened by a woman in her early forties. She had a very friendly face.

"Can I help you?" she asked the young girl standing outside.

"He's after me. You have to help me."

"Come in, come in. You're safe here."

She led the exhausted girl through to a cosy living room. A wood fire was burning in the corner. A man and a young boy were playing Scrabble on a table in the middle of the room. The man looked up from the board.

"William," his wife said. "This girl needs our help."

"My name's Jane," the girl was still out of breath. "There was a man after me."

"Twenty-six points," the boy screamed. "That's twenty-six points."

"Quail has a U, Billy," his father looked back at the board. "There's no such word as Qail."

"There is," he looked at the young girl, his eyes pleading. "There is such a word isn't there?"

"Billy," his mother said. "Be a love and put the kettle on. I'll be through in a while to help you."

Billy stood up and left the room. He was muttering something about twenty-six points.

"Take a seat," the man gestured to the sofa. "My name's William Landell and this is my wife, Lily. That Scrabble cheat in there is William Junior. What happened?"

"I was out walking. It's such a beautiful day. He came from nowhere and grabbed me from behind."

"Where was this?"

"About half a mile from the farm. He just appeared behind me and grabbed me by the shoulders. I managed to get away, but he chased after me. I thought he was going to kill me."

"We need to call the police," Lily said.

"Do you know who this man is?" her husband asked.

"No. He grabbed me from behind. I don't know where he came from. He almost caught up with me, but he must have tripped. I was so scared."

"So, you didn't see his face?"

"I only saw him when I turned around. I was running so I didn't get a good look at him. He was wearing a red sweatshirt – that's all I can remember."

"William," Lily said. "I'm going to call the police."

"OK," her husband agreed. "And I think we should let this girl's parents know what's happened. In the meantime, I'm going to have a look around outside. Maybe he's still lurking around."

"Don't go," Jane said. She looked terrified.

"I expect he'll be long gone by now," Lily assured her.

William Junior appeared in the doorway.

"Can you help me with the tray?" he asked his mother. "I always spill some."

Lily left the room and returned a few minutes later with a tray of tea and biscuits.

"Help yourself," she said to Jane, "The police are on their way. Where are you from?"

"Trotterdown. I mean London. We've only just moved here from London. My Dads just taken over as landlord at the Unicorn."
"James?" Lily said. "William knows him. I don't go in for drinking much, but William likes a game of poker and a few drinks every couple of weeks. You say you didn't recognise the man who chased you?"
"No. I only got a quick look at him."
"How old are you, love?" Lily asked her.
"Sixteen. Almost. I'm in the final year at school."
"This must be a far cry from London."
"I like it here. At least I did until today."
Landell came back in. "There's nobody there. He must have legged it."
"We'll catch him," his wife assured the young girl. "We can't have the likes of him wandering around these parts."

The police arrived half an hour later – two PCs in a car that looked like it hadn't been washed for months. Landell led them inside the living room.
"This is Jane," he pointed to the girl on the sofa.
"Jane Young," she said.
"Your Dads got the Unicorn, hasn't he?" the shorter of the two PCs said. "He seems alright."
"Tell them what happened," Landell said.
Jane told them about the attack.
"I didn't really get a good look at him. All I can tell you is he was wearing a red sweatshirt."
"We'll ask around," the taller PC said. "Let's get a statement, shall we?"
He took out a file and opened it up.
"Pete," Landell said to the short PC. "Let's have a look around outside while they're busy with the statement."

"I didn't want to say too much in there," the PC said to Landell as they walked across the field. "But we had a report of something similar two days ago."

"Go on," Landell said.

"A young lass was attacked on her way back from school. Some bloke came out of nowhere and grabbed her from behind. The bastard grabbed her breasts. She screamed, and he ran off. She couldn't give us much of a description either."

"What on earth is going on around here, Pete? This place used to be a safe place to live."

They carried on for half a mile or so but there was no sign of Jane Young's attacker.

"He's got to be stopped," Landell said as they walked back to the farmhouse. "He must be stopped."

CHAPTER ELEVEN

Harriet was the last to arrive at the farmhouse. She'd overslept. She hadn't taken any sleeping pills for months, and they'd affected her differently. Killian and the two Whites were talking to William Landell Junior outside the farmhouse. DS Duncan was nowhere to be seen.

"Sorry I'm late," Harriet said to Killian. "The alarm clock didn't go off."

"Are you alright?" the DI asked her. "You don't look too well. I hope you aren't coming down with Duncan's flu."

"I'm fine."

William Landell Junior looked even worse than Harriet. He looked like he hadn't slept at all.

"I appreciate that you're busy," Killian said to him. "We need to talk to everybody on the farm again."

"Busy?" Landell said. "I lost four more lambs last night. The ewes don't work nine-to-five, you know. Lambing time is a twenty-four hour job."

"I understand that. We can talk while you work. How's Gilly doing?"

"That's the reason I didn't sleep much. She was up most of the night with heartburn. I'll be glad when that baby pops out, I can tell you that. Nobody told me that having a baby would be so annoying."

You're all heart, Harriet thought.

"We'll try not to take up too much of your time," Killian said. He turned to Harriet. "Can I have a word?"

She followed him round to the back of the farmhouse.

"Are you alright?" Killian asked. "You don't look too well this morning. Flu is contagious, you know."

"It's not the flu. I didn't sleep much last night either. There must have been something in the air – a full moon or something."

She knew that was nonsense. The sleeping tablets hadn't worked like she'd remembered. She'd drifted in and out of sleep the whole night, and when it was time to get up, she felt like she hadn't slept at all.

"Littlemore called me first thing," Killian said. "It looks like he's found our murder weapon. One of the stones they examined had traces of blood on it."

"There was a lot of blood at the scene. How does he know it was the rock used to kill her?"

"The blood was concentrated and there were traces of hair and skin on it. Littlemore reckons it wasn't just one of the blood spatters."

"That's something at least."

"There's more. Littlemore pulled a partial print from the stone. It's being put through the database as we speak. I want fingerprints taken from everybody who works here at the farm. We'll save them the bother of having to go to the station. Thomas is going to take them here."

"Do you think the killer could be one of the farm workers?"

"They're all suspects. From what we've gathered, the murderer was close to the farm on Saturday morning. It could be one of them. Let's get started, shall we?"

Harriet and Killian spoke to Donovan Beech first. The stocky old farmhand was busy in the paddocks again. He was surrounded by sheep and lambs. He didn't even try to hide his displeasure when Killian and Harriet appeared at the fence. He scowled at Killian and looked Harriet up and down.

"I'm busy, in case you haven't noticed," he picked up a sheep and with astonishing strength he deposited her in the adjoining paddock.

"Mr Beech," Killian said. "We're all busy. We can talk to you while you work."

"Aren't those sheep heavy?" Harriet couldn't believe he could lift one over the fence.

"They probably weigh more than you do. I've been doing this for most of my life. You get hardened after a while. You wouldn't believe it to look at me, but I can still manage a five-minute mile, if I have to, that is. What do you want?"

"We're speaking to everyone on the farm again," Killian told him. "Some new information has come to light and we need to ask you all some more questions."

"Ask away," Beech filled a syringe with a milky liquid and injected it into the flank of one of the lambs.

"What's that for?" Harriet asked.

"Supplements. It gives them a bit of a boost. We can't afford to lose any of them. Did you come here to ask me about lambing? Are you considering a change of career?"

"No," Killian replied for her. "Can you remember what was happening on the farm on Saturday morning?"

"What do you think? Lambing. That's what was going on. I told you all this yesterday."

"Yesterday we spoke about Sunday. I'm asking about Saturday. Specifically, Saturday morning."

"Saturday, Sunday – it's all the same. The ewes have been popping them out like corks from a popgun."

"Can you talk us through Saturday morning?" Harriet said.

Beech injected another lamb. It let out such a high-pitched shriek that Harriet flinched.

"Sometimes you hit the nerve," Beech patted the lamb's rump. "It doesn't hurt them too much. Let's see. I got up late on Saturday. Around six if I can remember."

"That's late?" Harriet said.

"It is during lambing season. I'd only got to bed after midnight, so Landell allowed me a bit of a lie-in. I had a quick breakfast and came down here to the paddocks. I worked non-stop till lunchtime."

"You didn't take a break?" Killian said.

"Foot rot doesn't take a break, Inspector. No, I worked right through until lunch."

"Was there anybody else working here with you?" Harriet asked him.

"I prefer to work on my own. Are you accusing me of something? I didn't kill that French lass if that's what you're insinuating."

"We're not insinuating anything," Killian said. "You can't see the footpath from here – the house is in the way, but did you happen to see anybody hanging around here on Saturday?"

"I don't notice much when I'm clipping. Stubborn ewes and nail clippings in your face tend to take up most of your attention."

"We're going to need to take your fingerprints," Killian informed him. "One of my PCs will do it right here, so you're not interrupted in your work."

"I can save you the bother. If I'm not mistaken, you've already got them."

"Excuse me?"

"I had a bit of a run in with the law a few years back. An altercation at the Unicorn. I got off with a suspended, but my prints should be in your system somewhere."

"We'll take them anyway," Killian insisted. "Just to be sure."

"Do your worst. Now if you'll excuse me – I have to go and fetch some more formula. Somebody has to make sure there's roast lamb on your plates when you feel like it."

"What a horrible man," Harriet walked back towards the farmhouse with Killian. "He's strong though. Did you see how he lifted that sheep over the fence?"

"Farm life," Killian mused. "It toughens you."

"Enough to be able to chase a twenty-two-year old woman for over a mile?"

"Maybe. We'll compare his fingerprints with the ones Littlemore lifted from the rock, anyway. Let's have a chat with Tommy Dunn, shall we?"

Tommy Dunn was one of the temps – he was only called to the farm when the workload was too much. Lambing season was one of those times. He was taking a break when Killian and Harriet found him – he was sitting on a rock by a small pond smoking a cigarette.

"Mr Dunn?" Killian said. "We're glad we caught you on a break. Can we have a word?"

"Of course," Dunn was a tall, wiry man.

Harriet put his age at around twenty. He stubbed his cigarette out on the rock and lit another.

"Smoke?" he offered the pack to Harriet.

"No thanks. Have things calmed down a bit on the farm?"

"I've been at it non-stop since before first light. I'm due a break. What do you want to know? I'm just a temp. And I only spoke to you lot yesterday."

"Some new information has come to light," Killian told him. "Were you here on Saturday morning?"

"Of course. Mr Landell needs us all here this time of year."

"What were you doing on Saturday morning?"

"Mucking out mostly. The temps get all the glamorous jobs."

"Mucking out?"

"Cleaning up shit, if you want the technical term."

"Where was this?"

"All over. The cows and the pigs are the worst. Sheep shit hardly smells at all."

Harriet looked around. The pond was situated about fifty metres from the farmhouse. The cow sheds were roughly a hundred metres away. You could clearly see the rocks where the two bodies were found from there.

"Did you notice anybody hanging around on Saturday morning?" she asked him. "Somebody who wasn't supposed to be there?"

"No."

"Did you take a break at all?"

"I grabbed half an hour around nine, I think. It could've been a bit earlier."

"Where did you take the break?"

"Same place as always. I like it here by the pond."

"And you stayed here the whole time?"

"Beech likes to know where we are the whole time in case there's an emergency. Anything can happen on a farm. We need to be available to help at any time. Old Beech acts like he's Landell's second in charge, you see. I suppose it's because he's been here for donkey's years. He's a fine one to talk, though."

"What do you mean by that?" Killian asked.

"I mean he does what he pleases around here sometimes. I shouldn't really be telling you this, but he has a thing for the horses. It's a bit of an addiction if you ask me. Anyway, he buggered off on Saturday to get to the bookies in time to back a dead cert in the nine-fifteen at Doncaster."

"Are you saying Mr Beech wasn't here for a while on Saturday morning?"

"For about an hour. He went to Trotterdown at around eight-thirty to place his bet, and he came back an hour later."

CHAPTER TWELVE

1996

"Interview with Jurgen Weidmuller commenced 9:25," DI Andrew Snow said into the machine. "Present DI Snow, DS France and Mr Weidmuller's solicitor, Graham Dodds. Mr Weidmuller, do you understand why you're here?"
"Not really," the young Austrian had been picked up earlier that morning from the Youth Hostel in Trotterdown. His description matched that of a man who had carried out a number of indecent assaults on young girls. "You're making a huge mistake here."
"Jurgen," Dodds said. "Remember what we spoke about? You don't have to say anything."
"I haven't done anything. Why must I keep quiet?"
"OK, Mr Weidmuller," Snow said. "Three young girls have been assaulted in the space of a week. They were attacked by a man matching your description. At the times of all three assaults, you claim to have been out walking by yourself."
"Walking by myself isn't against the law in this country is it?"
"No, it isn't. But assaulting young girls is. Nobody can confirm you were out walking on those three occasions, and the attacker matched your description."
"Detective Inspector," Weidmuller's solicitor chipped in. "I've read the statements of all three girls. The description was rather vague if you ask me."
"All three girls mentioned a red sweater," the DI told him. "Your client openly admits to owning a red sweater."

"As do I," Dodds scoffed. "As do probably half the population of Trotterdown."

"What are you doing here in Trotterdown?" DS Snow asked.

"Backpacking," Weidmuller replied. "I'm making my way up north to John O Groats."

"Yet you've been here for over a week?"

"I like it here, and I'm in no rush. I don't know if you're aware of who my father is."

"No, I'm not."

"Let's just say that money isn't an object. My father is one of the richest men in Vienna. I'm taking a year out before I follow in his footsteps. You really do not want to take on my father if you know what's good for you."

"I'll take my chances."

The Austrian smiled a smug smile. DI Snow had a sudden urge to punch him in the nose.

"Is this going to take long?" Weidmuller asked. "I've got better things to do than sit in a dingy police station and answer dumb questions."

"I'm sure you have," Snow said. "Let me get this straight. You've been in Trotterdown for a week. Is that right?"

"About ten days," Weidmuller corrected him. "The views from the cliffs around here are breath-taking. I don't know how good your Geography is but Austria doesn't happen to have a coastline. Cornwall is so different from where I come from. Besides, the Youth Hostel is one of the best I've ever stayed at."

"Come on, Mr Weidmuller. A man matching your description was seen at the scene of all three assaults. You have no alibis for all three. Do you want to tell us what happened? Young girls? I can see how you might have been tempted."

"Inspector," Dodds interrupted him. "That's enough. I would strongly advise you to stop putting words in my client's mouth."

"Your client is suspected of sexually assaulting three young girls. We have enough evidence to charge him. I'm just trying to work out what made him do it."

DI Snow knew he was clutching at straws. A red sweater wouldn't be enough to stand up in court nor would the fact that Weidmuller had no alibis for the times the assaults took place.

The young Austrian kept quiet. The smug smile on his face widened.

"Do you think this is a joke?" Snow asked him.

"Yes. It's a farce if that's the correct word. You have no real evidence and you know it. My father knows nothing of this yet, but if you persist in this I'll have no option but to inform him, and believe me, you wouldn't want me to do that."

"Do you have a girlfriend, Mr Weidmuller?" DS France decided on a change of tack.

"No, not that it's any of your business. I tend to pick them up as I go along. I prefer it that way. No ties."

"Love 'em and leave 'em, then?"

"Excuse me?"

"Detectives," Dodds said. "This interrogation is leading nowhere, and you know it. It's obvious that my client didn't do the things you're accusing him of, so I suggest we wrap things up now."

"I'm not finished yet," DI Snow said, although he wasn't sure what else to ask the arrogant young Austrian.

* * *

"You let him go?" DI Snow had just finished telling one of the PC's who'd arrested Weidmuller about the interview.
"We had to," Snow sighed. "All we had on him was the red sweater, and the fact he didn't have an alibi. It's all circumstantial. You know as well as I do it won't hold up in court."
"I can't believe the smug bastard is free. It was him. I know it."
"I think so too but he isn't talking."
"I'm going to keep an eye on him anyway. We'll get him one way or another."

CHAPTER THIRTEEN

Donovan Beech's early morning visit to the bookkeepers in Trotterdown had been confirmed. It turned out that Beech was a regular there, and the manager remembered him being there just after opening time on Saturday morning. The horse he'd backed hadn't exactly performed as he'd hoped – it had limped in second from last.
"Beech was in there for less than five minutes," Killian said to Harriet outside. "He placed his bet and left. Tommy Dunn told us he was gone for an hour. What was he doing for the rest of the time?"
"And why did he lie to us? He said he was at the farm all morning."
Killian scratched his head. "He was gone for an hour. If he left the bookies in Trotterdown at eight-thirty, it's possible he could have driven back to the farm, killed Lauren Moreau and returned to work."
"She was killed a good few miles from Trotterdown," Harriet pointed out. "How would Beech even know she would be on the path?"
"Maybe he saw her in Trotterdown. Maybe she didn't leave at seven after all. Maybe she had some breakfast or a cup of coffee before she set off. She set off a bit later, and Beech saw her. He knows the area well. He'd have known roughly where she would end up by the time he got back to the farm. Maybe he planned it all on the drive back."
"All these maybes are driving me crazy," Harriet said. "It's all speculation. We don't have anything concrete to go on."
"Littlemore is checking the fingerprint on the rock against the ones we got from everybody on the farm this morning, including Donovan Beech's. Beech was right – his fingerprints were already on our system. He beat the crap out of a bloke who was hassling a young woman in the Unicorn a few years ago."
"I didn't have him pegged as a knight in shining armour."

"That's how he got off with a suspended sentence. The woman spoke up for him. Anyway, we'll know more when the prints have been checked."

Harriet and Killian drove towards the station. Harriet had a splitting headache. Her head felt like it was being crushed in a vice.

"Do you have any headache tablets?" she asked Killian.

"In the glove compartment. I keep some there for Megan. She gets regular headaches."

"How's Megan doing?" Harriet found the tablets and swallowed two of them.

"She can remember our wedding day like it happened yesterday – it's a memory she seems especially keen to hold on to. She can recall the dress she wore – the ill-fitting suit I had on, she even remembers the fight afterwards. Two of her brothers had a bit of a disagreement about something. But she doesn't even know who I am sometimes. It's as if the memories of the past are more real to her than things that are happening today, if that makes any sense."

"Do you still have somebody to help out?"

"I went against all the advice I was given, and I decided to try and do it myself – neither Megan nor I really like having a stranger in the house, but I don't know how much longer I can do it. It's draining. It sounds terrible, but I sometimes think it would have been easier if she'd been in a car accident and was paralysed instead. At least then her mind would still be OK."

Harriet's headache was gone by the time they parked outside the station. The tablets had worked.

"Littlemore's here," Killian pointed to the head of forensics' Ford Granada. "That could mean good news – he only comes in person when he has something important for us."

"Let's hope so," Harriet knew all too well that the odds of clearing up a murder investigation became much greater the more time passed.

The face of the head of forensics didn't look like it belonged to the bearer of good news. Littlemore was waiting in Killian's office with his head in his hands.

"Jack," he looked up and nodded to the DI. "Harriet. Do you want to close the door?"

"What's going on, Alan?" Killian closed the door and sat down.

"A balls-up, that's what's going on. The fingerprint we pulled from the rock has been identified."

"And?"

"And the owner of the finger it came from is Frankie Lewis. Twenty-four years old and, if it were up to me, he'd soon be an ex-forensics technician."

"One of your team?" Harriet couldn't believe it.

"Young Frankie may have forgotten to wear gloves when he handled the rock in the lab. The idiot can't even remember. I came straight here to tell you in person. It's an embarrassment to the whole department."

"Mistakes happen, Alan," Killian said. "We're only human. Don't be too hard on him."

"Frankie Lewis has wasted all our time - yours included, and he's not getting off lightly. Could I ask you to keep this between us, though?"

"Of course," Killian agreed.

Harriet nodded her head. "It won't go any further."

"Thank you," Littlemore looked relieved. "I'm going to take a slow drive up the coast. It'll give me some time to think of a suitable punishment for young Mr Lewis."

"So, now we know even less than we did this morning," Harriet said when Littlemore had left the office. "We've got nothing from the interviews with the people on the farm and the fingerprint on the rock is a dead end. I can't believe a forensic technician could be so stupid."
"We're all only human," Killian said again. "Like I said, mistakes happen. I'm calling a case meeting in half an hour. We don't have any concrete evidence, so what do we concentrate on now?"
"Motive," Harriet said without thinking.
"Yes. That old chestnut. Why? Why does somebody follow a young woman, kill her and dump her body by some rocks?"

CHAPTER FOURTEEN

"Why, why, why?" was a familiar mantra of Killian's.
Harriet and the two PC's White had lost count of how many times they'd heard the DI utter those words.
"What motivates somebody to want to kill?"
"There was no suggestion of any sexual assault," Harriet began. "So, we can rule that out."
"Hatred," Eric said. "Fear or financial gain."
"Nobody knew the woman around here," Thomas pointed out. "Why would anybody fear or hate her? And what kind of financial gain could be achieved by killing a young French student?"
"Maybe she had life insurance," Eric suggested.
"She had no family," Harriet said. "Apart from a brother she didn't speak to. Maybe her boyfriend stood to gain if she died."
"We'll look into it," Killian said.
"Maybe it was the brother," Thomas said. "Why didn't they speak to each other? Maybe they hated each other. Enough for him to want to kill her."
Maybe, maybe, maybe, Harriet thought. *Maybe* was quickly becoming her least favourite word.

"OK," Killian said. "We've covered the classic motives for murder, and we've got something new to look at. Harriet, I want you and Eric to have another word with the Frenchman. He told us he's planning on sticking around until Friday. Find out about Lauren's brother. There may be something there that ties in with all of this. Ask him where he was on Saturday morning, too. Thomas, see if you can find out if she took out some kind of life insurance policy and find out who stands to gain in the event of her death."

"How am I supposed to do that?" Thomas asked.

"You're a policeman, Thomas. Use your brain. We have the dead girl's name and date of birth. Our relationship with the French police is very good. I've always found them to be cooperative in the past. I'm going to have another chat with William Landell Junior."

"What for?" Harriet asked.

"Two bodies were found on his farm yesterday morning. I've known the Landells for years. I knew his father well. Maybe young William will open up more with a one-on-one chat."

"Do you think he knows something about the bodies?"

"If he does, I'll find out. Let's get to it."

* * *

Harriet and Eric found Jean Dupont in his usual place in the Courtyard of the Backpackers. He was talking to somebody on his mobile phone. Harriet's command of French was sketchy – she'd done a few years of the subject at school and forgotten most of what she'd learned, but she did remember one word. Mort – dead.

Jean Dupont ended the call and shook his head.

"I spoke to Lauren's brother, Philippe. His sister is dead, and he doesn't seem to give a hoot."

"I'm sorry," was all Harriet could think of to say.

"We live in a sorry world," the earlier arrogance was gone. "He told me to make the necessary arrangements myself. Do you know when Lauren's body will be released?"

"That all depends," Eric replied. "It depends on whether we find any further evidence and need to do another autopsy."

"I want to give her a decent send off."

"Will her body be going back to France?" Harriet asked.

"No. I've thought about it and there's nothing left for her in France – especially now her brother doesn't seem to care. Lauren loved the sea. I wonder if I'd be allowed to let her ashes be blown up in the wind and out into the Atlantic Ocean. It is, after all, something France and England share. Do you think I'd be allowed to do that?"

"I'm sure it can be arranged," Harriet said. "We need to ask you a few more questions. Do you know if Lauren had any life insurance?"

"Lauren?" Jean looked like he was going to burst out laughing. "I'm sorry. Lauren was a free spirit. She wasn't one to look that far into the future."

That's one avenue closed then, Harriet thought.

"Are you sure she didn't have any policies?" Eric asked.

"No, but I do. I've always been the cautious one. The boring one, Lauren used to say. I have insurance against just about everything – death, ill health, dread disease. My father taught me to insure against every possible scenario."

"If you don't mind me asking, Mr Dupont," Harriet said. "Who would be the beneficiary, should anything happen to you?"

"Lauren, of course. I took out a small policy about six months ago. Things were going well between us, and it was starting to get serious. I took out a policy in case anything happened to me. And vice versa."

"You took out a life policy on Lauren?"

"Of course. It's not a substantial amount – a hundred thousand Euros, but it's enough to make everything a bit more bearable."

Not a substantial amount? This changes everything.

"You stand to gain a hundred grand?" Eric exclaimed.

"I didn't kill her for the insurance money, if that's what you're thinking."

"Mr Dupont," Harriet said. "Don't you think it's strange to take out a policy on a healthy, twenty-two-year old woman?"

"Not at all. Anyway, I didn't kill her. Now, I believe it's your job to prove otherwise."

The Frenchman's self-assurance had returned.

"Good luck with that," he wasn't finished yet. "I have an alibi for Sunday, in case it's slipped your minds."

"What about Saturday?" Eric asked him. "Where were you on Saturday morning?"

"In bed, mostly. I can't remember. What's Saturday morning got to do with anything?"

"Can anybody confirm where you were on Saturday morning or not?"

"No. I was in bed alone. I got up around ten or eleven. I believe I told you this yesterday."

"A decent size insurance policy," Eric said. "No alibi for Saturday morning. A hundred thousand Euros is a lot of money."

"Why do you keep on mentioning Saturday morning? You said Lauren was killed on Sunday."

"We did," Harriet said. "But now we have reason to believe she was attacked on Saturday. Let's just say some new evidence has come to light. Nobody can put you here on Saturday. Is that right?"

"No. I mean, I was here. I didn't go out until around lunchtime."

"Where did you go?" Eric asked.

"I caught the bus into Polgarrow. It's a small village a few miles from here."

"I know where it is."

"I had some lunch in a pub there. A few drinks, and then I got the bus back. The bus driver will probably remember me."

"Mr Dupont," Eric said. "We're not interested in Saturday afternoon. Maybe something's getting lost in translation here. Nobody can vouch for your whereabouts on Saturday morning. For all we know, you could've followed her along the path, attacked her and come back here. A hundred thousand Euros is quite an incentive."

"You're out of your mind. I loved Lauren. I was the only one who did. I could never kill her for money."

"The insurance company probably won't pay out until this is all over, anyway," Harriet pointed out. "They're always very reluctant when a death is suspicious."

"I think I should call my lawyer," Jean Dupont cast Harriet a defiant glare.

"I think that might be a good idea," she wasn't fazed by his veiled threat. "The insurance policy changes everything. We're also going to need to get hold of Lauren's brother. Whether he cares or not – he's still technically the next of kin."

"Philippe? Why do you need to get hold of Philippe? He's a dog."

"Just routine," Eric told him. "We'll be in touch again, Mr Dupont." He looked at Harriet and then back at the Frenchman. "I'd get hold of that lawyer of yours as soon as I could if I were you."

CHAPTER FIFTEEN

"Do you think he did it?" Eric asked Harriet as they drove away from the Backpackers.

"The life insurance policy is a bit dodgy if you ask me. Who takes out a hundred thousand Euro policy on a woman of Lauren's age?"

"It is a bit odd. I don't like him anyway. The threat of a lawyer backfired, too. We were quite a team back there. I like working with you. Where are you going? The station is in the opposite direction."

"Hospital," Harriet turned right and joined the main road.

"You're going to see that beanpole pathologist, aren't you? The DI isn't going to be too impressed. We're supposed to be working."

"This is work, Eric."

"Whatever you say. Have you always gone for tall blokes?"

"I want to find out about the other body," Harriet ignored his question. "Dr Finch ought to have finished with the examination."

"Why are you so interested in a mummy?"

"Aren't you curious about he ended up there?"

"Not really. It's probably just an old tramp. There used to be loads of them around in the old days. He probably crawled into the rocks one winter night to keep warm and froze to death. Nobody seemed to miss him, did they?"

"What if it wasn't an old tramp?"

"So what? It was ages ago. We're probably not obliged to investigate, anyway. What's that thing? Statute of liability?"

"Limitations, Eric," Harriet corrected him. "Statute of limitations. And if you were familiar with the law, you'd know there is no statute of limitations in this country for serious offences. I read about a murder case where the killer was caught over thirty years after he killed an old lady."

"I'm a policeman, not a lawyer and I still think you're wasting your time with an old corpse."

Harriet knocked on Dr Finch's office door.

"Come in," Finch shouted from inside.

Harriet and Eric entered the office. The expression on the lanky pathologist's face on seeing Harriet made Eric chuckle. Dr Finch was beaming from ear to ear and his blue eyes sparkled.

"Harriet," he said. "And PC White. Is it Eric or Thomas? I always get confused. You two look so similar."

"We do not," Eric looked rather insulted. "I'm Eric."

"Sit down," Finch said. "What can I do for you?"

"Have you had a chance to examine the other body yet?" Harriet asked him.

"I'm just busy writing up the report. It was a rather interesting examination."

"My colleague here seems to think he was just an old tramp seeking refuge for the night."

"Old bugger gets out of the cold wind on a winter night," Eric elaborated. "And freezes to death. It can get pretty Baltic out there in the middle of winter."

"I'm sorry to disappoint you," Finch said. "But our man was neither old nor did he freeze to death."

"How *did* he die?" Harriet asked.

"I found three massive fractures to his skull, along with a number of minor ones. I'd say he was repeatedly bashed over the head with something very hard."

"You said he wasn't old," Eric said. "How can you tell?"

"His teeth are the teeth of a young man's. Teeth are ground down over time. I'd say he was still in his twenties when he died."
"You can tell after all this time?" Eric was amazed.
"That and much more. The hair that was still attached to his scalp told us he had dark brown hair when he died. The follicles don't lie."
"Do you know how long he was buried in the rocks?" Harriet said.
"That's harder to tell. Even though he was partially hidden, the elements will have got to him, as will a number of small animals and much smaller micro-organisms."
"There goes my appetite," Eric said.
"A rough guess?" Harriet urged.
"At least fifteen years. Probably more."
"Fifteen years? That puts it at around the turn of the century. Did you find anything else?"
"Do you want to have a look for yourself?"
"Yes, I do," Harriet answered without thinking.
"I'll give it a miss if it's alright with you," Eric quickly added. "My stomach is already feeling a bit iffy. I think I'll get a coffee from the canteen."

"Nothing fazes you does it?" Finch and Harriet walked down the corridor. "You're not afraid of anything the sea can throw at you and now you want to have a look at the body of a man who's definitely seen better days."
"I'm curious, that's all. And I seem to be the only one who is. Killian keeps pushing it aside as though it doesn't concern us."
"Maybe he's right."
"You said he was murdered. We can't just ignore it."
"It was a long time ago, Harriet," Finch pushed open the door and put his hands on her shoulders.

"I don't think this is the time or the place for that sort of thing," she looked up into his eyes.

"I have to warn you," Finch ignored her flippancy. "Littlemore and the fire department did their best to get him out in one piece but quite a bit of him refused to budge. There's a fair chunk of him missing."

"I'm ready," Harriet took a deep breath. "He's the victim of a crime, nothing more."

Finch hadn't been exaggerating. From the size of the bulge under the sheet on the metal table in the examination room, Harriet could tell straight away that a lot of what was once a young man was still stuck to the rocks at Landell's Farm. Finch removed the sheet and Harriet gulped. She could feel the bile collecting in her throat. She held her breath for a few seconds and exhaled.

"Are you alright?" Finch asked.

"Where's his head?"

"Unfortunately, it came off when they were excavating the rocks around him. I would've removed it anyway to examine it properly."

The severely decomposed body on the table didn't even resemble a man. Both arms had somehow been cemented to the body and all that distinguished them as arms were two skeletal hands that stuck out from the lower torso like fins on a fish. Denim trousers appeared to have kept some of the flesh on the legs reasonably intact, but the socks had been eaten away and two fleshless ankles ended in a pair of large boots. The boots had withstood the path of time remarkably well.

"They're obviously good boots," Harriet observed. "I bet they were quite expensive."

"They've lasted well," Finch agreed.

"I suppose Littlemore will want them now you've finished."

"What for?"

"The boots could give us some idea who the poor bugger is. They're very unusual boots."

"Nobody's mentioned anything about examining the boots to me."

"What's wrong with everybody?" Harriet still couldn't believe there was a dead man lying on a table in the mortuary, and nobody was showing any interest in how he ended up there. "The man was murdered for God's sake – whether he was killed fifteen years ago or fifty shouldn't matter. Doesn't anybody care?"

"Harriet," Finch put his hand on her shoulder. "Calm down." She was getting quite worked up.

"Sorry, maybe you're right. We should be focusing on the French girl anyway. What are your plans for this evening?"

"That's entirely up to you."

"There's a band on at the Unicorn at eight thirty. They're supposed to be very good."

"A band? I think my rock n roll days are over."

"Come on. They play all sorts. Besides, you said it was up to me."

"OK," Finch smiled. "I'll meet you there at half-seven."

"You might even enjoy it," Harriet took out her phone and switched on the camera.

She took a series of photographs of the boots attached to the dead man on the table.

"Harriet," Finch said. "Leave it alone."

"Please, just humour me – I'm curious." She put the phone back in her pocket. "I'll see you later."

Finch shook his head, leaned down and kissed her on the top of her head.

CHAPTER SIXTEEN

"What was it like?" Eric White asked Harriet.
Eric was halfway through his second cup of coffee in the canteen at the hospital.
"There's not much left of him."
"Urgh. We're not going to find out who he is. You realise that don't you?"
"He was wearing a very unusual pair of boots."
"You're hoping to get an ID from a pair of boots? You're even crazier than I thought. No, I reckon our mummy is going to remain a mystery forever."
"Drink up," Harriet ordered. "Let's go and see what the rest of the team has come up with."
"Frenchie is odds on favourite for me."
"I don't know. I still don't think he has the stamina to chase someone for over a mile."
"We'll see. Killian's going to want to formally interview him. I bet the slimy bastard has already been on the phone to his lawyer."

* * *

Harriet and Eric arrived at the station the same time as Killian. The DI looked exhausted. His face was haggard, and he looked extremely anguished.
"Are you alright?" Harriet asked him. "Did something happen with William Landell Junior? Does he know something about the bodies?"
"No, I only had chance to have a brief chat with him. His wife seems to be stressing him out a bit. I don't know much about pregnant women – Megan and I couldn't have children, but she was screaming like a banshee when I got there. Poor Landell's taking a bit of strain."

"Hormones," Harriet said. "You men wouldn't understand. I don't think you realise what having a baby does to a woman."

"Anyway, he claims to have no idea about either of the bodies, and I believe him. Landell's a good man. His father was too. No, I've been at home for the past couple of hours. Megan keeps phoning me and hanging up. She doesn't even remember doing it. She accused me of lying to her. I don't know what I'm going to do."

"Do you need some time off?"

"It might come to that. I could get another carer in but that's always been my last resort."

"Go home," Harriet ordered. "I can head up the case meeting."

"Are you sure?"

"Of course. We found something very interesting from our chat with Jean Dupont. Six months ago, he took out a life insurance policy on Lauren Moreau – a hundred thousand Euro policy."

"I'd say a hundred grand is a good motive for murder," Eric chipped in.

"A definite motive," Killian agreed. "I want the Frenchman brought in again."

"He threatened us with his lawyer," Eric told him.

"Good. Let him come in with his lawyer. What harm can it do?"

"Go home," Harriet said again. "I can handle this."

"Duncan's due back tomorrow. At least then we'll have a full team again. I'll see you in the morning."

Harriet watched him drive away.

"He's not himself," Eric observed. "It must be terrible. It sounds awful, but I reckon if I ever end up like his wife, I'd rather somebody put me out of my misery."

"She has her good days, Eric. Go and find Thomas. Tell him about the meeting. Seeing as though there's just the three of us, we may as well have it in the canteen."

* * *

"She didn't have any policies," Thomas White informed Harriet and Eric in the canteen. "I couldn't find anything."

"There wasn't anything in her name," Harriet said. "But her boyfriend took out a policy on her six months ago. It was for a hundred thousand Euros."

"A hundred grand? That's a lot of money."

"And a good motive for killing her," Eric added.

"Did you find out about her brother?"

"Philippe Moreau," Harriet said. "We have his contact details, but I don't expect to get much from him. He and Lauren didn't seem to be on speaking terms. He wasn't even bothered about her death when Jean phoned him."

"What do we do now?" Thomas asked.

"We're going to interview Mr Dupont tomorrow. His lawyer should be here by then."

"It was him," Eric insisted. "It has to be him."

"We'll try and get him to crack tomorrow. As I've been put in charge temporarily, I want to move on to the other body."

"What for?" Eric asked.

"Because he was murdered on our patch and it's our job to investigate."

"Harriet's beanpole showed her the body," Eric told Thomas.

"And they say romance is dead," Thomas quipped. "What are you going to do for a second date? Cultivate maggots together?"

"Autopsy replays over a nice bottle of red wine?" Eric suggested.

"That's enough, you two. The dead man was wearing a pair of unusual boots" Harriet took out her phone and showed them the photos she'd taken earlier.

"You can't see much on there," Eric pointed out.

"Hold on," Thomas stood up and left the room.

He returned with his laptop. He connected it to Harriet's phone, and a photograph of the boots filled the screen.

"Is that..." Eric said. "Is that what's left of his legs?"

"That's disgusting," Thomas added.

"Look at the boots," Harriet said.

"Can you zoom in?" Eric asked. "There's a label there next to the laces. I can't quite see what it says."

Thomas enlarged the photo and the label became easier to read.

"There on the tag," Eric pointed. "It says Wonderlite."

"It's Wanderlust," Thomas corrected him. "Wanderlust."

"Wanderlust," Harriet said. "I've never heard of it."

"It means a desire to travel," Thomas explained. "It's German."

"Can I say something?" Eric asked. "What exactly are you hoping to achieve here? Surely you can't expect to find out who the dead bloke is from a pair of old boots?"

"It's a start, Eric," Harriet insisted. "We have to start somewhere."

"We're wasting our time."

"Ninety percent of the time we spend at work is wasted," Harriet said. "But we keep going, don't we?"

"I still don't see why you're so obsessed with a fifteen-year old corpse."

"I'm not obsessed."

"Wanderlust," Thomas interrupted the argument. "I've found it. It was a brand of hiking clothing and equipment in the nineties. They manufactured boots, gloves, clothing and climbing equipment. They closed down in 1998."

"1998?" Harriet spoke directly to Eric. "There you are, we've already found out something."

"Have we?" Eric was none the wiser.

"Eric, 1998 is nineteen years ago. If Wanderlust closed in 1998 it means our man bought the boots before that. It gives us a better timeline to concentrate on."

"Harriet, a good pair of boots can last years. I don't see how that helps us."

"Jon Finch put the time of death sometime between fifteen and twenty years ago – we now know when they stopped manufacturing those boots, so we can at least narrow it down a bit."

"They had a factory in Freiburg," Thomas scrolled down the screen. "And there's a photo of the boots here."

All three of them looked at the photograph on the screen. There was no doubt about it – They were the same boots the dead man was wearing.

"They were part of the Wanderlust Mark 4 line," Thomas read.

"And, they cost over three thousand Deutsche Marks," Eric pointed to the screen. "Whatever that means."

"I think the Mark was about three to the pound in the nineties," Thomas said.

"A thousand quid for a pair of boots," Eric exclaimed. "That's a lot of money, even today. It still doesn't give us anything to go on though."

"I reckon he was a foreigner," Harriet thought out loud. "That's probably why he wasn't missed at the time. Possibly German if the boots are anything to go on. German, twenty something years of age. It gives us somewhere to start."

"No it doesn't," Eric argued. "What are we supposed to do? Check out every German who came into the country in the nineties? It'll take years to check."

"He might not even be German," Thomas added. "He could've bought the boots over the Internet."

"Internet shopping wasn't that popular in the nineties," Harriet said.

"Are we done yet?" Eric was clearly getting irritated. "We'll interrogate Frenchie tomorrow and see what crops up. We're wasting our time on the other one."

"OK," Harriet didn't feel like arguing anymore. "I'll see you both tomorrow. I've got a date in a couple of hours."

"Where's the Doc taking you this time?" Eric asked. "A romantic trip on the Ghost Train?"

"See you tomorrow."

CHAPTER SEVENTEEN

Jon Finch was already there when Harriet arrived at the Unicorn. He'd managed to secure a table in the middle of the room – close enough to be able to see the band, but not too close that they'd be deafened by the noise.

"Harriet," Finch stood up and beckoned to the chair opposite him. "You look lovely. Can I get you a drink?"

"I feel like a glass of wine."

"What's the occasion? You don't drink."

"I don't know. I just feel like a glass of wine for some reason."

"Coming up then. Red or white?"

"Surprise me."

Finch placed a glass of red wine on the table and sat down. "Red's much better for you. What time is the band going on?"

"Half-eight, I think. They're supposed to be very good."

She took a tentative sip of the wine and smiled. It had been a very long time since she'd tasted alcohol, and it felt strangely decadent. She took a larger sip.

"Good?" Finch watched her savour the wine.

"Very good. You're a bad influence on me, Dr Finch. You bring out the dark side in me."

"Rubbish. I'm getting to know you. That dark side of you comes out whenever it pleases you. Especially on the boat."

"Speaking of the boat," Harriet drained the rest of the glass in one go. "When can we go out again?"

"I've got a few days off coming up. We can go out sometime over the weekend. The forecast doesn't look too rosy though. There's a front

coming in from the west on Friday. It looks quite nasty."
"Perfect," she looked at the empty glass. "That went down quite well."
Finch started to laugh. "I'll get you another one."

The Unicorn was slowly filling up. Harriet looked around the bar, and realised she recognised just about everybody in the pub. She'd only been in Trotterdown just over a year, but in that time, she'd got to know just about all of its residents.
"There you go," Finch put another glass of wine on the table.
The band were tuning up on the small stage. There were four of them – a singer, a guitarist, bass player and drummer.
"Here goes," Finch looked at the musicians. "It's been a while since I watched a live band."
"Just go with the flow," Harriet said and started to giggle.
The first glass of wine had gone straight to her head.
"Your eyes are different when you've had a drink," Finch said. "They're full of mischief."
"It's you. I told you, you bring out the dark side in..."
A drum roll and a crash of a cymbal drowned out Harriet's voice. The band had started their first song.

An hour and three glasses of wine later, Harriet was feeling very drunk. She knew there would be no way she'd be able to drive home.
"They were brilliant," she articulated the words slowly.
It took a great effort to be able to say three words.
"Just what the doctor ordered," she added.
"The doctor is advising you to drink a glass of water," Finch said.
"You're so boring," Harriet said and burped. "Sorry, maybe you're right. I need to go to the loo."
She stood up and grabbed the top of the chair just in time.
"I'm alright," she insisted and staggered to the toilets.

She looked at herself in the mirror in the Ladies. Her cheeks were flushed, and her eyes were slightly glazed over.

"You're drunk," she admonished her reflection. "Harriet Taylor, you're rat-arsed."

This was followed by a fit of laughter. An old woman came in and Harriet tried to regain her composure. She couldn't stop laughing.

"Are you OK?" the woman asked her.

"I'm a bit drunk."

"Good for you, love," the woman said and locked the door to the cubicle.

Harriet made her way back to the table.

"Is that for me?" she pointed to a glass of tonic water and lemon. "Thanks." She took a long sip and spilled half of it down her cheek. Finch took out a handkerchief and wiped her face.

"You're kind," Harriet said. "Danny wasn't kind, but you are."

"Do you want to go home? I'll drive you – I've only had a couple of pints."

"The band has another set to play. I'm fine. You're kind. Danny was a real bastard. I was such a fool." Her head lurched forward.

"You're not a fool," Finch said. "You are one of the most amazing women I've ever met."

"How many women have you met?"

"Not many," Finch admitted.

"Ha," Harriet said so loud that half of the people in the bar turned to stare at her. "Sorry." She addressed the room.

The drummer played four steady beats on the snare drum to announce the second set was about to begin. Harriet sat back in her chair, and a huge grin spread across her face.

CHAPTER EIGHTEEN

1996

The band started to play their second set. The Unicorn was packed to the brim. Half of Trotterdown had turned up – it wasn't often they had a chance to watch a live band, and this one was reputed to be very entertaining. The loud music didn't stop the four men sitting at the table in the far corner of the room from enjoying their regular Friday night poker game.

"I'm out," James Young placed his cards face down on the table. "That's too rich for me."

James was the newly appointed landlord of the Unicorn.

"Too rich for you?" William Landell remarked. "Look at this place tonight – you're making a fortune. The whole town's here. I'll raise five quid." He took a long sip of his shandy. "Any offers? Pete?"

"What the hell," Pete put a five-pound note on the table. "Call."

"That's a bit beyond my budget," the fourth man at the table threw his cards on the pile.

His name was Andy Booth and he had recently retired from the Post Office.

"I'm on pension," he added. "And my Martha will kill me if I blow it all on a poker game. Another round?"

"Put it on my tab," James offered.

The game of poker was getting quite exciting by the time Booth returned with the drinks. William Landell was guarding his cards like his life depended on it.

"What's it to be, Pete?" he said. "It's going to cost you fifty quid. Or you could fold."

Pete looked at the pile of money on the table and then looked at his cards. He took out his wallet and emptied the contents on the table. "Forty-six quid," he said. "I'll have to owe you the other four."
"That's good enough for me. What have you got?"
Pete smiled and placed the king of hearts on the table. He did the same with the kings of spades and diamonds.
"Three kings," he said. "Read 'em and weep."
Landell looked at the three kings on the table.
"Two pairs," he put a pair of twos down.
"Yes," Pete raised a fist in the air.
"And another pair of twos." Landell had four of a kind.
"What the hell?" Pete stared at Landell's cards and the pile of banknotes on the table. "I'm going to have to do a week of overtime to make that back."
"You still owe me four quid," Landell reminded him and started to scoop up the cash. "Next round's on me."

  The band had slowed things down a bit. They were playing a low-tempo number, and a few couples had got up to dance. They were dancing close together. One of the couples - a young man with brown hair and a blonde woman were taking the slow dance very seriously. The man had his hands on the woman's backside and his head on her shoulder. His eyes were closed, and he seemed lost in the music. The couple swayed in time with the beat and didn't even seem to notice when the band stopped playing. Eventually, they were the only ones left on the makeshift dance floor.

  "Pete," Landell said. "Isn't that the Austrian bloke? Look at him. He's acting like he owns the place."
James Young stood up. "I'm not having the likes of him in my pub."

"Careful, James," Pete warned. "He hasn't done anything."

"We all know that's not true," James said and walked over to the man who was still holding his partner tightly on the floor.

"You," he slammed his hand down on the man's shoulders. "Out. I'll not tolerate perverts in my pub."

The band stopped playing, and the room went quiet. All eyes were on the scene that was playing out on the dance floor.

"Is there a problem?" the Austrian let go of his partner and smiled at the landlord.

"There will be a problem if you don't leave. And by leave, I mean leave town. If you know what's good for you, I mean."

"I don't think so," the Austrian smiled a smug smile. "I like it here. Why would I leave when there are so many pretty girls around?"

James's fists clenched, and Pete reached him just in time.

"James," he said. "Calm down. He's not worth it. You could lose everything."

James realised that Pete was right – an assault in front of so many people would certainly mean he would lose his license.

"Look at him," he said. "He's acting like nothing's happened."
He had been persuaded to return to the table.

"He attacked my baby girl," he added. "And he's in my pub acting like he's the bee's knees."

"The police had to let him go," Landell said. "They had no choice. They didn't have enough on him."

"He's a rich kid," Pete said. "His Dad's some millionaire in Vienna. He thinks money gives him immunity."

"That's me done for the night," the retired Post Office worker drained his beer. "My Martha gets all stroppy if I get home late."

"Same time next week, Andy?" Landell asked him. "I'm on a winning streak."

"Same time next week," Andy agreed and left the table.

"He's making my blood boil," James Young stared at the young Austrian who was now dancing with a different woman.

"His time will come," Landell said. "His time will come. You mark my words."

CHAPTER NINETEEN

When Harriet woke up her head felt like someone was playing the tuba in it. She opened her eyes and flinched. The sunlight coming through the gap in the curtains was stabbing into her brain. She sat up in bed, and the throbbing in her head got worse. She didn't know where she was. She had a vague memory of a band playing at the Unicorn, but she couldn't remember anything more than that. She looked around the small room. She was lying on a single bed. There was a chest of drawers against one wall and an arm chair sat next to the window. She got out of bed. There was a glass of water on the bedside table. She picked it up and downed it in one go.
Where am I?

She made her way downstairs. Jon Finch handed her a cup of hot, black tea.
"Morning," he said. "I trust you slept well?"
"I slept," she took a sip of the tea and winced. "What on earth is this stuff?"
"Green tea. It'll help to detox your system a bit. You had a fair bit to drink last night."
"I can't remember much of last night. I didn't make a fool out of myself, did I?"
"Not really. Your unusual dancing had the whole pub entertained for a while."
"Oh my God. I wasn't that bad, was I?"
"I'm just kidding. Alcohol seems to open up the old truth ducts, though."

"What do you mean?"

"German boots," Finch said. "You wouldn't stop going on about a pair of unusual German boots."

"The boots," Harriet remembered now. "The company that manufactured them closed down in 1998. It means our mystery man bought the boots at least nineteen years ago."

"Nineteen years?" Finch was suddenly interested. "How did you find all this out?"

"The good old Internet. They were made by a company that called themselves Wanderlust. They manufactured luxury hiking and climbing equipment. Those boots cost the equivalent of a thousand pounds back in the late nineties."

"A thousand pounds for a pair of boots?"

"I'm going to do a bit more digging when I get the chance. Right now, I'm late, and we have a smug Frenchman to interview."

"I have to be at the hospital at eight. I can drop you off at home if you like."

* * *

Harriet kissed Finch goodbye and went inside her house. A cold shower was in order. She went upstairs, turned on the cold tap and stepped underneath the icy jets. Within seconds her whole body felt numb. She quickly washed, got out and towelled herself off. She felt a bit better after the shower, but her head was still throbbing.

Never again, she thought. *What on earth made me drink so much last night?*

She made some tea and swallowed two headache tablets. She was going to be very late.

* * *

Killian's face told Harriet immediately the DI was less than impressed that she was over an hour late.
"That's two days in a row now," he said. "What's going on with you, Harriet? You never used to be late."
"I'm having trouble sleeping," she lied.
"Jean Dupont is in one of the interview rooms. His lawyer arrived late last night and he's not happy."
"I'm sorry. Where's the rest of the team?"
"Duncan called in sick again. He really didn't sound well. The two Whites are picking up Donovan Beech from the farm. Your tardiness has put us behind schedule."
"I'm sorry," Harriet said once more. "It won't happen again."
Killian was right – Harriet was rarely late without a good reason.
No more alcohol for me, she thought, *not for a very long time.*
"Can we get started then?" Killian asked her.
"Of course."

Jean Dupont was sitting next to his lawyer in interview room two. Harriet thought the smile on his face seemed even smugger than it had done before. The presence of his lawyer seemed to bring out his arrogance even further.
"DC Taylor had to attend to an urgent matter," Killian lied. "I appreciate you've come a long way." He addressed the French lawyer. "Let's get started, shall we?"

Dupont's lawyer looked far too young to be a qualified lawyer. He had smooth skin and bright eyes. His suit jacket was slightly crumpled – he looked like he'd travelled all the way from France in it and not changed.

"Interview with Jean Dupont started at 9:35," Killian said after turning on the recording device. "Present, DI Killian, DC Taylor and Mr Dupont's legal representation. It's Mr Petit isn't it?"

"Petit," the lawyer corrected him. He didn't pronounce the T at the end. "It's a common mistake amongst Englishmen."

"Sorry, Petit. Mr Dupont, do you understand why you're here?"

"Incompetence," Dupont sat back in his chair and folded his arms." His lawyer nodded in agreement.

"Before we begin," Petit said. "I understand my client isn't under arrest?"

"That's right," Killian said.

"And he is here voluntarily?"

"Also correct. We merely want to ask Mr Dupont some more questions in the light of some new information we've received."

"By new information I assume you're referring to the matter of a fairly innocuous life insurance policy my client took out on his girlfriend?"

"Innocuous?" Harriet joined in, "I'd hardly call a hundred thousand Euros innocuous. It's a lot of money."

She'd done a calculation. With the current exchange rate, it equated to almost eighty thousand pounds. Hardly a meagre amount.

"My client has briefed me on the details surrounding Lauren Moreau's death," Petit said. "And as far as I can tell there is nothing to link my client with the scene of the crime, nor is there any reason why he would want her dead."

"Apart from a hundred thousand Euros," Harriet reminded him.

"The policy was taken out over six months ago. I'm sure you're also aware that Mademoiselle Moreau would also have benefited if anything were to happen to my client. The life insurance was for both their sakes. You have no concrete evidence against Mr Dupont – the insurance policy is, how do you say it? – Clutching at the straws."

"Mr Petit," Killian said. "A young French woman was brutally murdered. We have reason to believe her body was dumped while she was still alive, and she remained conscious for over twenty-four hours."

Jean Dupont sat forward in his chair. This was apparently news to him.

"She was still alive when she was buried by the rocks?" he said.

"We believe so. And I'm sure you'll also agree that we all want the same thing here. We want to get to the bottom of all this." He looked at Dupont's lawyer. "If your client has something he wants to tell us, surely it's best to hear it sooner rather than later."

"Nice try, Inspector," Petit tapped his finger on the tablet in front of him. "I'm not an idiot. All the evidence you have against my client is circumstantial. And if he did kill his girlfriend, why is he still here? Why didn't he run? He could quite easily have disappeared."

Killian knew the young lawyer was right. All they had was a life insurance policy and a lack of an alibi for Saturday morning. Dupont had stuck around – it was now four days since the attack – he could've been miles away by now if he'd wanted to be.

"Like I said, Mr Petit, we just want to get to the bottom of this. It's our job."

Harriet cringed at Killian's last comment. They were getting desperate and the fresh-faced lawyer knew it.

"Let's go right back to the beginning, shall we?" she suggested.

"Lauren left the Backpackers at seven on Saturday morning. A woman walking her dog a mile from Trotterdown saw her an hour or so later. She wasn't seen again until William Landell Junior's wife found her body by the farm on Monday morning. We believe that Lauren was attacked later on Saturday morning. We found her rucksack a mile or so away from Landell's Farm, and we have evidence to suggest a struggle took place. It appears that she ran towards the farm but didn't make it."

Dupont's lawyer said something to his client and Dupont started to laugh.

"Could you share the joke in English please?" Killian asked. "For the record."

"Of course," Petit said. "I simply asked my client when he was last in the gym. He's not as fit as he used to be. I very much doubt he could run very fast."

"Lauren was a much better runner than me," Dupont admitted. "She was the athlete, not me."

Harriet had suspected this. She couldn't imagine the chain-smoking Frenchman being able to outrun his girlfriend.

Petit looked at his watch.

"I'm a busy man. Let me summarise what we have so far if I may. All you have is an innocent life insurance policy. You have nothing to suggest that my client was anywhere near the farm that day. No fingerprints, boot prints or shreds of clothing belonging to Mr Dupont – nothing. I assume you've checked for traces of blood on his clothes.

"Of course," that was one of the first things Killian had insisted on and they'd found nothing.

"He could've easily got rid of the clothes he was wearing," Harriet pointed out.

"You have nothing. I suggest you leave my client in peace to mourn the loss of his girlfriend."

Killian turned off the recording device. The interview had been a complete waste of time. All Dupont's lawyer had succeeded in doing was to reinforce what they already suspected – Jean Dupont wasn't their murderer.

CHAPTER TWENTY

Donovan Beech was next in line to be interviewed. Eric and Thomas White had collected him from Landell's Farm. Beech was understandably displeased.

"I've got work to do on the farm," he told Killian in the interview room Jean Dupont and his lawyer had recently vacated. "The ewes are popping them out like mad at the moment. Landell can't afford to be short staffed."

"We appreciate that," Killian told him. "But we've also got work to do. We're investigating a murder. It can't be helped."

"I've already told you everything. Twice. What's up with you lot? Don't you take it in the first time?"

"You forgot to mention the part about your little detour to the Bookkeepers in Trotterdown," Harriet reminded him.

"Who told you about that?"

"That's not important," Killian said. "Why did you say you hadn't left the farm on Saturday morning? You were gone for over an hour."

"I'd been working non-stop for hours. I reckoned I deserved a bit of time off to go and place a bet. I'd been given a good tip."

"Why did it take you an hour to place the bet?" Harriet asked him. "We spoke to the Bookkeeper, and he said you were in and out in less than five minutes."

"I picked up some supplies while I was there. Surely you don't think I had something to do with the death of that foreign lass?"

"That's what we're trying to find out," Killian said. "And I don't like being lied to. It tends to arouse my suspicions."

"Come on, I placed the bet and stopped off at the supermarket to get a few things in. I bought some food and a couple of bottles of scotch. I don't get out to Trotterdown much and I thought I'd kill two birds with one stone. Susan will be able to confirm it."

"Susan?" Harriet said.

"She works the checkout at the supermarket. We chatted for a while. Her old man's got a touch of the flu. Speak to her she'll confirm it."

"We'll check it out," Killian was starting to think this was the second time that morning they had hit a brick wall. "What time did you get back to the farm?"

"Around half-nine. I work twice as fast of the rest of them there, so I figured I was entitled to an hour off to go into town."

"How long have you worked on the farm?" Harriet asked him.

"All my life. I was born in one of the fields, remember. I dropped out of school at fourteen and started working for old Landell. He didn't seem to mind that I was so young. I was never the academic type anyway – I was much better with my hands."

"So, you were there in the nineties?"

"That's right."

"Do you remember much about those days?"

"I'm not a brain box, but I still have it up here," he tapped his head. "I have a good memory. I remember the first girl I kissed back in 82, and I remember the first calf I helped to bring into the world. I was sixteen years old."

"Can you remember anything strange happening in the late nineties? Something to do with a young German man?"

"Harriet," Killian said. "That's enough. I think Mr Beech has told us what we need to know."

"German you say?" Beech scratched his head. "No, it doesn't ring a bell."

"He would have been in his early twenties back then," Harriet added.

"I said that's enough," Killian said again. "Mr Beech, you're free to go. We may need to speak to you again."

"I thought you might say that. You lot always say that, don't you? You know where to find me." He stood up and left the room.

"What the hell was that about?" Killian asked Harriet when they were alone in the interview room.

"He was at the farm in the nineties. He might know something about the body buried in the rocks."

"And you thought you'd just casually bring it up while we're in the middle of interviewing him about another murder?"

"Why not? Don't you want to know who the dead man is?"

"Of course, but as I've told you it's going to have to wait. A fifteen-year old corpse isn't a priority at the moment. How many times do I have to spell it out to you?"

"Nineteen," Harriet corrected him. "He died at least nineteen years ago."

She told him what she'd found out about the boots he'd been wearing.

"Nineteen, fifteen, it's neither here nor there. Until the murder of the French woman is cleared up it's out of bounds."

"But..."

"But nothing. Leave it alone. We have our hands full with the Lauren Moreau murder. Our two main suspects have been practically ruled out, and once again we're back to square one."

"We still haven't checked Beech's story about the supermarket."

"We will, but he was telling the truth. He didn't do this – I can feel it in my gut. We'll have a briefing at noon. I want to concentrate on the motive once more. It's all we have. There will be no more snooping around in the case of a man who's been dead for nearly twenty years. Do I make myself clear?"

"Of course," Harriet tried to sound as convincing as possible. Her curiosity was roused, and she knew she wouldn't be able to let it lie.

"I mean it, Harriet."

"I said OK."

"Did you catch the newspapers this morning?" Killian changed the subject.

"I got up late. I didn't have chance to look at them."

"It's not good. The locals were kinder, but the dailies are hinting that we're not taking it seriously because the victim was a foreigner."

"That's nonsense. We've been working round the clock."

"You and I know that. Tanya, the press officer warned me that something like this could happen."

"It's ridiculous. We treat all murders the same – whether the victim is British, French or Chinese."

"It's what sells newspapers, I'm afraid. The general public have become so blasé with murder that the press put any spin on it they can. The Super is worried it might tarnish our reputation. You know how he gets?"

"Why can't they just leave us alone to do our jobs?"

"It's the way of the world, I'm afraid."

Harriet's headache was rearing its ugly head again.

"I need a cup of tea."

"You've got twenty minutes. And I want fresh minds at the briefing. We need to come up with something fast – the press is already breathing down Superintendent Lemon's neck and you know very well what a knock-on effect that has."

Harriet knew all too well. She knew that when the diminutive Superintendent was harassed, he made it Killian's problem and that problem inevitably filtered down to the officers on the ground – Harriet, the Whites and the absent DS Duncan.

CHAPTER TWENTY ONE

1996

Jane Young had never had a detention before. She looked at the clock on the wall – 4:30. Half an hour to go. The clock appeared to have slowed down. She was sure it was 4:30 a few minutes ago. She wasn't looking forward to explaining to her Dad the reason for being late home. It hadn't even been her fault. It was a simple case of being in the wrong place at the wrong time. A group of girls had been smoking at the back of the science lab, and Jane had happened to be there just after they'd left. Old stickler Steinway had appeared, smelled the smoke in the air, and put two and two together and come up with five. Now, Jane was staring at the clock in the history room waiting for the minute hand to reach the top.

"You can go," Steinway announced. "And don't let me catch you smoking again. That's what living in a pub does for you. It's not a healthy environment for a young girl, you know."

Jane didn't even try to defend herself. She'd always found it hard to stand up for right and wrong. Besides, she wanted to get out of there as quickly as possible. She put on her coat and headed for the door.

"It's a terrible habit," Steinway called after her. "Give it up now, if you know what's good for you."

* * *

The streets of Trotterdown were deserted as Jane made her way towards the Unicorn pub. She turned left onto Pier Street and breathed in the fresh sea air. The wind had picked up and the salty breeze blowing in from the sea made her shiver. She put her hands in her pockets and increased her speed. She knew her Dad would be furious about the detention, but she wanted to get home and out of the wind as soon as possible.

"Excuse me," a voice came from nowhere and Jane jumped. "Sorry if I scared you but I'm lost."
The young man who'd appeared from nowhere had a strange accent. He was wearing a black beanie and a pair of sunglasses.
"Is it always this cold around here?" he asked. "I'm trying to find The Backpackers."
"It's back towards the harbour," Jane pointed and carried on walking.

Jane was a few hundred metres from the Unicorn when she heard a noise up ahead. It was coming from the small service road that ran down the back of a row of terraced houses. She quickened her pace. She'd just about passed the service road when she heard the noise again – it sounded like the shuffling of feet. Then, somebody grabbed hold of her from behind. She tried to scream, but the hand over her mouth prevented the sound from getting out. The arm around her neck was very strong, and she found herself being pulled into the single lane road.
"I've got a knife," her attacker told her calmly, and moved his hand down to one of her breasts.
His other hand was still covering her mouth.
"Do as I say, and I won't harm you, OK?"
For some reason, Jane found herself thinking about something that had happened in London. It was a few years back – also when she was on her way back home from school. She'd been walking home with a friend when three boys had appeared and started making lewd suggestions. Without thinking, her friend kicked one of the boys so hard between the legs, his scream was probably heard all over the

city. Jane had wished back then she'd had the guts to do something like that.

But she knew she didn't have it in her, not then, or now.

"I said OK?" the man said again, louder this time.

Jane nodded frantically. She just wanted to go home. The man's hand still cupped one of her breasts, and the sweet smell of the aftershave on the hand over her mouth was making her feel sick.

"I'm going to take my hand away from your mouth now. If you scream, I'll kill you. Do you understand?"

Jane nodded again.

He slowly removed the hand and placed it on the waistline of her school trousers.

Her Dad would be wondering where she was by now.

"You're very beautiful. Do as I say and remember I have a knife." He pulled her trousers down in one swift motion and she screamed. She didn't know where the scream came from. She screamed like she'd never screamed before.

"Bitch." He took out the knife and stabbed her in the stomach twice in quick succession.

She fell to the ground and put her hand on her stomach. Her attacker walked down the access road. He seemed to be walking in slow motion. She watched him as he removed his beanie.

Dad will come and find me.

The blood had soaked her shirt, but she didn't feel any pain.

I'm fine. I'm going to be fine. I stood up to him. For the first time in my life, I stood up to somebody.

Dad will be here soon.

CHAPTER TWENTY TWO

"Donovan Beech's story checked out," Killian told Harriet and the Whites in his office. "I spoke to that Susan woman at the supermarket. Beech bought some groceries and a couple of bottles of cheap scotch on Saturday morning. He paid by credit card. The time on the slip puts him there at 9:15. It looks like he left the bookies just after half eight, spent a while in the supermarket, and paid at a quarter past nine. There's no way he could have been anywhere near where Lauren Moreau's body was found."

"So, what now?" Eric asked. "Asterix the Gaul has been ruled out and so has Beech."

"Motive," Harriet got there before the DI.

"That's right," Killian said. "Why does somebody kill a young woman? A woman who's out hiking? Was it a spur of the moment thing? Did she happen to meet someone along the way or was it carefully planned in advance?"

"Who knew she would be there at that time?" Harriet said.

"Apart from her boyfriend, you mean?" Thomas said.

"Apart from her boyfriend," Killian repeated. "As far as we're aware, only Jean Dupont knew she was doing the coast-to-coast, so that would suggest a spur of the moment killing and I don't have to tell you that's going to make our jobs much more difficult. Any ideas? I don't care how far-fetched they are - let's throw a few theories around, shall we?"

The room was silent. None of the team appeared to have any suggestions.

"Nothing at all?" Killian urged.

Harriet stared out the window. There wasn't a cloud in the sky, nor a breath of wind in the air. She thought about the promise of a day out on Dr Finch's boat. Finch had warned of a nasty weather front on the way, but the prospect merely excited her. Fighting against the wind out on the open ocean made her feel alive.

"Harriet," Killian broke her reverie. "What are you thinking?"

"Trotterdown."

"What about it?"

"We've been concentrating all our efforts on Trotterdown and Landell's Farm which is less than five miles away."

"Do you have any other suggestions?"

"Yes," something had occurred to her while she'd been thinking about Finch's boat. "If we re-examine the facts – the woman walking her dog, the place where the attack took place, and the spot where her body was found it strikes me that we need to look in the opposite direction."

"She's right," Eric had cottoned on to Harriet's line of thinking. "If this was a spur of the moment thing, Lauren's murderer was probably coming from the other direction when he bumped into her."

"Grubton," Harriet said. "It's where the coast-to-coast trail starts."

"Or even Crayford," Thomas suggested. "It's half way."

"The killer could have even been doing the coast-to-coast," Harriet continued. "From Grubton to Trotterdown. He comes across Lauren Moreau, something happens, and he kills her."

"The coast-to-coast is a forty-mile hike," Killian said. "A two-day hike. Twenty miles a day. How long do you reckon it takes to walk twenty miles?"

"The trail is pretty level," Thomas informed them. "There's very few inclines. I reckon at a steady pace you could do four miles an hour. If you don't stop, I mean."

"So, five hours then – maybe six if you stop for a few breathers," Killian said. "It still doesn't make sense. For someone to get to where Lauren was attacked they would've had to leave Crayford at four in the morning on Saturday. It was freezing on Saturday morning. Who in their right mind would do that?"

"It takes all sorts," Thomas mused.

"We've got something to look at now," Killian said. "It's a start. We'll check out Grubton and Crayford. Find out if anybody stayed at those two places on Thursday or Friday last week."

"There's also a campsite in between Crayford and Landell's farm," Eric informed them. "We used to camp there when I was a kid. I'm sure it's still going. Maybe the killer stayed there."

"Good," Killian said. "Now we're starting to use our heads. We'll check it out."

"I don't want to put a dampener on things," Harriet said. "But even if we do find out that somebody was staying in Grubton, Crayford or at the campsite, they'll be long gone by now. Today's Wednesday. It's been two days since Gilly Landell found Lauren's body."

"We might get a name," Thomas remained optimistic.

"And there can't be many people doing the hike this time of year," Eric added. "Once we have a name we can bring them in and interrogate them."

"We interview them, Eric," Killian found himself smiling. "We're not the Gestapo."

"Whatever. We have the fingerprint Littlemore pulled from the rock. All we need to do is match that fingerprint with the finger it came from."

"The fingerprint's a dead end," Killian cast Harriet a knowing glance. They'd agreed to keep Littlemore's technician's blunder quiet.
"Thomas, you and I will go to Grubton and Crayford. Harriet, you and Eric can ask around at the campsite."
"Is Duncan ever coming back to work?" Eric asked.
"When he's well again," Killian said. "He sounded much better when I spoke to him on the phone this morning. With any luck he'll be fighting fit, and back at work tomorrow."
"I actually miss the grumpy bugger," Thomas admitted. "He's a bit stuck in his ways, but what you see is what you get with old Duncan."
"Let's get onto it," Killian looked at his watch. "We'll meet back here at four to go over what we've found."

CHAPTER TWENTY THREE

The name Grubton didn't do the quaint little fishing village justice. Killian parked his car in the car park in front of the harbour and gazed out into Grubton Bay. The harbour was quiet – the few fishing boats that still plied their trade in the waters there were already far out to sea. Killian had a list of places to look in Grubton. That list numbered two – The Grubton Arms and a B&B around the corner from it. Grubton wasn't exactly on the tourist map. Its main claim to fame came from its location at the start of the coast-to-coast trail.

"I've never been here before," Thomas said as they got out of the car. "It's very pretty. I wonder who decided to call it Grubton – it's hardly an appetising name is it?"

"No," Killian agreed. "The Grubton Arms is one of only two places to stay here. Let's see what they can tell us shall we?"

From the outside, the Grubton Arms wasn't much to look at. If it weren't for the sign hanging above the doorway, you wouldn't even know it was a hotel. Killian and Thomas went inside. An elderly woman was solving a crossword behind what Killian assumed was the reception desk. She looked up as they approached.

"Afternoon," she frowned at the sight of Thomas's uniform. "Is there something wrong?"

"Good afternoon," Killian said. "We're from Trotterdown police. DI Killian and PC White. Could we ask you a few questions?"

"Detective Inspector?" she seemed impressed. "Could I ask you a question first?"

"Go on," Killian was confused.

"Throw Georgia, mumbled the pig."

"Excuse me?"

"Throw Georgia, mumbled the pig. Seven letters. Second letter is an A. It's a crossword clue."

"I'm sorry, I don't really go in for crosswords."

"Is this about the French girl? It's all in here," she tapped the newspaper on the desk in front of her.

"It is. It's quiet around here. Did you have anybody staying here on Thursday or Friday last week?"

"No. We haven't had anybody stay since the middle of February – some mad Pole who wanted to do the coast-to-coast in winter, but we haven't had anybody since. There's an Australian couple booked in for two days from tonight. That's the only reason I'm here now. They should be here any minute."

"So nobody has stayed here since mid-February?"

"Not one. It's a bit early in the season. Come end of April we'll be busier but, unless you're doing the hike, there's not much here for the tourists. They all want their fancy amenities these days."

"I expect the B&B will be the same," Thomas asked her.

"I expect so. We don't really talk much – me and Mr Fingley. He owns the B&B. We're his only competition, and he tends to take things very seriously, but you can ask him. Would you mind mentioning to him that we have a party of ten booked in for tonight? Just for a bit of fun?"

"I'll see what I can do," Killian smiled.

"Warthog!" Thomas exclaimed as they walked round the corner towards the B&B.

"What are you going on about?" Killian said. "Have you lost your mind, man?"

"Throw Georgia, mumbled the pig. Warthog – it's an anagram. The crossword clue."

"Now you've got that off your chest, let's see if Mr Fingley can tell us anything."

The letters *B&B* were written in writing so small above the door to Mr Fingley's house that Killian was surprised he got any business at all. He rang the bell, and shortly afterwards a tall thin man stood in the doorway. He had blonde hair that obviously wasn't his – the wig was so badly fitted, Thomas had to try hard not to laugh.

"You're from the police," he said. "What's up? Is this about the whelks?"

"Whelks?" Killian said. "No, it's not about the whelks. Can we come inside?"

Fingley led them inside to a spotlessly clean reception room. "Take a seat," he gestured towards a two-seater couch against the window. "Would you care for something to drink? A cup of tea or maybe a drop of sherry?"

"No, thank you," Killian spoke for himself and Thomas. "Mr Fingley, have you had anybody staying here in the past week? We're especially interested in Thursday and Friday last week."

"No, alas, I haven't. It's quiet in these parts at this time of year. It's March and I don't advertise much. I prefer to go with word of mouth – one tends to get a much more desirable clientele that way, wouldn't you agree? What's this all about? I must admit when I saw you in the uniform." He nodded to PC White. "I was sure it was about the whelks."

"What happened with the whelks?" Thomas asked and from the expression on the DI's face, immediately wished he'd kept his mouth shut.

Killian looked quite annoyed.

"A couple of weeks ago, I bought some whelks from one of the fishermen down by the harbour. One should be able to treat oneself now and again, I'm sure you'll both agree."

Here we go, Killian thought.

"Anyway, to cut a long story short, that tyrant down at the harbour assured me they were whelks but when I got them home and opened up the tub you wouldn't believe what I found in there."

The suspense is killing me.

"Mussels, that's what. Mussels. I couldn't quite believe it. Surely there has to be a law against that kind of thing? I reported it of course, but I haven't heard anything since. You can imagine how disappointed I was when I found mussels instead of whelks. I love a good whelk. Mussels just aren't the same. Are you sure you won't partake in a drop of sherry?"

Bring me the whole bottle, for God's sake.

"No," Killian said. "We won't take up anymore of your time."

He couldn't bear to listen to the man's waffle any longer.

"I'm sure business will pick up soon," he added. "I heard that the lady who runs the Grubton Arms has a party of ten booked for the whole week."

He left Mr Fingley sitting there with his mouth wide open.

"Why did you have to ask him about those damn whelks?" Killian asked Thomas as they walked back to the car.

"Sorry, sir. I didn't think he was going to go on about it all day. Did you see his face when you told him there were ten people staying at the Grubton Arms?"

"He deserved it. Remind me never to recommend his B&B to anybody in the future."

* * *

The guest house in Crayford yielded similar results. Killian and Thomas White learned that Lauren Moreau was the only person who had booked to stay in the past week, and she hadn't turned up. Killian and Thomas knew that already.
"Hopefully Harriet and Eric have had better luck at the campsite," Thomas said as they drove back to Trotterdown.
"It's the logical choice." Killian swerved to avoid a pothole in the road. "From there, the killer would have only had to set off at seven, seven thirty to get to where Lauren was attacked by nine."

CHAPTER TWENTY FOUR

The Brackenwood resort was hardly doing a roaring trade. A total of two tents were pitched in the huge open grounds. Harriet wondered if they were wasting their time. She'd just finished on the phone with Killian and the DI had informed her that, apart from finding out that Grubton housed a number of eccentric individuals they'd come up with nothing relevant to the investigation.

"This place has changed," Eric observed. "When we used to come here when I was a kid all they had was an ablution block and a tiny office cum general store. They've even got a swimming pool now. I bet they're packed out in the summer."

They made their way towards what Harriet assumed must be the reception office. It was a newly painted building. A large shop stood next to it. The shop was closed.

"They've even got a pub," Eric added. "The Brackenwood Arms. Things have really changed. I might even consider taking a holiday here when the weather gets warmer."

They went inside the office. A bored-looking young woman was watering the plants on the windowsill.

"Good afternoon," Harriet said to her. "Could we have a word?"

The woman looked at Eric in his uniform, and at Harriet. "Is something wrong?"

"No. We'd just like to ask you about somebody who may have been staying here last week. On Thursday or Friday to be more specific."

"That ought to take all of five seconds. I'm Rose. It hasn't exactly been busy lately."

She went behind the desk and looked at the computer screen.

"There was a couple of Scots here the whole of last week. They booked one of the statics."

"Statics?" Eric said.

"Caravans. They're really fancy. And Graham was here from Wednesday until Saturday. I don't get him – he comes here the same time each year. Same four days every year. He does the coast-to-coast. Sometimes he starts in Grubton, other times, Trotterdown. You'd think he'd be bored of it by now. He always stays here in his tent."

"Do you have his details?" Harriet asked.

"Hold on," Rose clicked the mouse. "Graham Wilde. He's forty-eight years old from London. I suppose it must be nice to get out of the city for a while."

"Do you know where he might be now?"

"He left here early on Saturday morning. He was packed up and gone by the time I arrived here at eight. I think he was planning on heading south down to Land's End. He walks like a steam train – I've never seen anything like it."

Harriet and Eric left the resort with the contact details for Graham Wilde. Eric tried ringing his mobile, but it went straight to voicemail.

"What do I say?" he covered the handset and looked at Harriet.

"Tell him the truth. Tell him that we need to speak to him as a potential witness. His presence is required at the police station in Trotterdown."

Eric repeated what Harriet had said into the phone and rang off.

"Do you think he'll turn up?" Eric asked.

"You can never tell. If he's got nothing to hide why wouldn't he? If he doesn't show, we'll have to try and find him."

"If he left the campsite before eight on Saturday morning that would put him where Lauren Moreau's body was found at the time we think she was dumped there. I reckon he was heading that way. Trotterdown is an ideal place to go through if you're heading south. He could've bumped into the French woman on the way. Pretty girl – he tries it on, she's having none of it, so he kills her."

"Let's see what he has to say for himself before we start speculating, shall we?"

* * *

She parked outside the station and they went inside. A very pale-faced DS Duncan was talking to a young PC at the front desk.

"Afternoon, Sarge," Eric said. "Are you feeling better?"

"Not really," Duncan sniffed. "But I can't handle it at home any longer. The wife is driving me mad. She keeps pouring God knows what down my neck and it's not helping. I'm better off at work. Any new developments in the investigation?"

"We have a new lead," Harriet told him about Graham Wilde. "He left the campsite early on Saturday morning. If he walked in the direction of Trotterdown, he would've been by Landell's farm the time we think Lauren Moreau was killed."

"That's something at least," Duncan took out a handkerchief and blew his nose. "Where is he now?"

"He's not answering his phone," Eric told him. "I left a message telling him to get here as soon as possible."

"If he did kill her, you know that's not going to happen?"

"Then we'll go and find him," Harriet said. "We also found something interesting about the other body."

"Other body?"

"The one that had been there for years. The boots he was wearing were made by a company that closed its doors in 1998 which means he bought the boots at least nineteen years ago."

"What of it? Leave it alone. We're not going to get anywhere with that one."

"But..."

"But nothing. Forget about it. The Super won't thank you for wasting time on a dead-end. We have the murder of a French national to figure out. You know how the press gets when a foreigner is killed on our patch?"

Harriet knew that Duncan was probably right, but she couldn't forget about a man who'd been buried at Landell's farm for all that time. Her curiosity wouldn't allow it.

"Aren't you even interested as to how he ended up there?" she asked the DS.

"Leave it, Harriet," he glared at her. "That's an order."

Killian walked down the corridor towards them.

"Peter," he observed Duncan's pallid complexion. "Are you sure you're well enough to come back to work?"

"I'm fine. Harriet and Eric have just been filling me in on the investigation."

"Ah, yes. Graham Wilde. Has he been in touch yet?"

"Not yet," Eric said. "But I only phoned him a short while ago."

"If he left the camping grounds on Saturday morning he could be in Land's End by now," Harriet pointed out.

"We'll find him," the DI assured her. "He's our only lead at the moment. We'll find him."

CHAPTER TWENTY FIVE

Graham Wilde turned out to be a hard man to find. Harriet and the team had contacted every campsite, hotel, B&B and Backpackers from Trotterdown to John O Groats, and they'd come up with nothing. Graham Wilde hadn't stayed in any of them.

"We've got his details from his mobile phone company," Thomas said. "Graham Wilde. Forty-eight years old. Apparently, he works as a legal clerk at a small solicitor firm in the city."

"Is he on our system anywhere?" Eric asked.

"The DS is busy with it."

"What about his workplace," Harriet said.

"I spoke to them," Eric said. "They weren't too pleased to receive a call from the police, but Wilde hasn't been seen at work since last week. He takes the same week off every year. They last saw him last Thursday."

"It's Wednesday today," Thomas pointed out. "That means he's due back at work tomorrow."

"How does that help us?"

"Think. If he doesn't show up at work tomorrow, then he's got something to hide."

"I wish it were that simple," Harriet mused. "We still have the task of finding the man."

DI Killian walked in.

"I take it you've had no joy in finding our mystery hiker? Those faces tell it all."

"We've got nothing, boss," Harriet told him. "We've checked all possible accommodation from here to the tip of the country. Mr Wilde didn't stay at any of them. He hasn't been seen since he left the campsite in Crayford on Saturday morning."

"Mmm. He's not answering his phone – nobody's seen him for four days, there's something strange going on here. Do we know how he got here from London in the first place?"

"I spoke to one of his work colleagues," Thomas said. "He follows the same routine every year. He gets the train to Exeter then hops on a couple of local buses to get to Grubton. He's a man of habits by all accounts."

"Check the train records," the DI ordered.

"What for?" Eric said. "You don't need to give out any ID to buy a train ticket."

"Check them anyway. Do we have a photograph of the man?"

"The law firm he works for said they'd email one through," Thomas said. "They weren't too impressed about the whole thing."

"I don't care," Killian said. "We need to put his photo out. Somebody must have seen him. Get onto it. Train records, Eric."

Eric left the room.

DS Duncan came in the room with a rare smile on his face.

"You're suddenly feeling better," Killian said. "Did you find something?"

"Our Mr Wilde has a few skeletons in his closet," Duncan told him.

"Go on."

"He's got a record. He was done for drink driving a few years back. But it's the other charge that's the interesting one. Sexual misdemeanor.

"Sexual misdemeanor?" Harriet and Thomas said at the same time.

"Eighteen months ago," Duncan continued. "He was in a pub in London, and it seems he went a bit too far with a young lass there. He was charged but got off with a suspended. I suppose it pays to work for a bunch of lawyers."

"Right," Killian said. "That puts a whole new perspective on things. We'll need to go over that misdemeanor case. Thomas, that's a job for you, and see if that law firm have sent through that photograph. Good work, Peter."

DS Duncan smiled, and his nose twitched. His eyes began to water and the sneeze that followed made everybody jump.

"Go home," Killian told him. "The last thing we need right now is for us all to come down with whatever lurgy you've got."

"But, Jack," the DS protested.

"Go home and get some rest. I'll give you a ring if we need you."

Duncan took out a handkerchief, blew his nose and left the room.

"How on earth did this bloke get off with a suspended?" Thomas said to Harriet in his office.

They were sitting in front of Thomas' computer looking at the case report for Wilde's sexual assault.

"29th September," Harriet read. "The accused was seen by 3 witnesses in the Lion on the Old Kent Road. Three different people claimed to have witnessed Graham Wilde pestering a twenty-year old woman at the bar. He kept at it for almost an hour. Later, he was seen following her to the toilets. It was inside the toilets where the assault took place. One of the bar staff heard a scream and went to investigate. She found Graham Wilde and a very distraught young woman inside the ladies toilet."

"I still don't see how he escaped jail time," Thomas said.

"Nobody actually witnessed the assault. It was her word against his."

"But he was found inside the ladies toilets."

"His lawyer argued that his advances weren't spurned – the woman in question had a bit of a reputation if you know what I mean. Those legal minds no doubt brought her character into question. They probably tore the poor woman to pieces on the stand."

An email came through. It was the photograph Graham Wilde's employers had promised to send,
"He doesn't look like a pervert," Thomas noted.
"What's that supposed to mean?" Harriet said.
"He looks quite normal to me." He printed the photograph and laid it on the desk.
Graham Wilde had a thin face, a very pointy nose and close-set eyes. His hair was thin and receding and turning grey at the sideburns.
"He looks like a pervert to me," Eric White was standing behind them.
"What did you find out about him?"
"He got away with fondling a young woman in the ladies," Thomas told him.
"He's the one then. We've found our killer. It has to be him."
"Eric," Harriet said. "Let's not jump the gun here. We need to put all our efforts into finding him."
Eric looked closely at the photograph. "It's him. He probably walked right past the French woman, liked what he saw and tried it on. She blew him off, so he attacked her."
"Eric," Harriet raised her voice. "Stop speculating. We need to find him. Only then can we be sure. What did you find from the train records?"
"I'm still waiting. They said they'd email them over if they find anything."
"Speed them up a bit. We need to find this man."

The train records yielded results. Graham Wilde had purchased his tickets online. Eric was beaming from ear to ear when he handed the sheet of paper to Killian.

"He booked the tickets three weeks ago," the DI read. "He's due to travel back to London on the 5:15 from Exeter."

Harriet looked at her watch. "That's in less than two hours. If we leave now we might be able to catch him before he gets on that train."

"Take Eric with you," Killian said.

Harriet drove far too quickly up the A30 towards Exeter. Her GPS informed her that it would take her just over an hour to get there. Eric pointed to the speedometer. "You're going to get a speeding fine. There's cameras everywhere on this road."

"We need to get there before Wilde gets on that train. It can't be helped."

Harriet eased off on the accelerator slightly. "Is that better?"

"Slightly. Do you think this Wilde bloke is our killer?"

"Part of me wishes he is. Then we can put this one to bed and concentrate on the other body."

"You can't let that one lie, can you?"

"I'm intrigued, that's all – it's a real mystery. Aren't you even a little bit curious as to how he ended up there?"

"Police car up ahead," he warned. "Of course, I'm curious but I doubt if we'll find out much after all these years."

Harriet ignored the warning and drove at eighty miles per hour past the police car. She glanced in her rear-view mirror – the police car didn't appear to have registered her speed.

A sign on the road told them they were 5 miles away from Exeter. "Duncan told me to stay away from the body we found in the rocks. He was furious. I don't know what's wrong with him."

"His flu is probably making him even more cantankerous than usual," Eric said. "Let's see what we get out of this Graham Wilde character, *then* we can figure out if it's worth looking into the other body. The train station is just outside the city centre. I haven't been here in years.

The impressive Exeter St David's station had stood for over 150 years. Harriet was immediately impressed by the grandeur of the building. She found parking round the corner and she and Eric got out the car.

Eric looked at his watch. "We made it just in time. We've got ten minutes before the train leaves for London."

They hurried inside, and Harriet looked up at the board that displayed the arrivals and departures.

"Platform 1," she said.

"It's that way," Eric pointed past a small café.

"Do you have the photograph?"

"Of course. Graham Wilde shouldn't be too hard to spot – he's got quite a distinctive face."

They were in luck. A man matching Wilde's description was sitting on a bench on the platform. He was reading a book. Harriet looked at the photograph.

"That's him," she said. "That's definitely him. There's no mistaking that nose and the close-set eyes."

Wilde looked up from his book as they approached.

"Mr Wilde?' Harriet asked him.

He placed his book on the bench next to him. It was a reference book about birds. "Is there something wrong?"

"Mr Wilde," Harriet said again. "We need you to come with us back to Trotterdown. There are some questions we need to ask you."

"But I have a train to catch. I have to be back at work tomorrow."

"That can't be helped," Eric said. "Could you please come with us?"

"Am I being arrested?"

"Not at the moment," Harriet told him. "But we do need you to come with us. As I said there are some questions that need to be answered."

"Why didn't you return my call?" Eric asked Wilde as they drove back to Trotterdown. "I left a message for you to contact us."

"I lost it," Wilde replied. "Somewhere between Grubton and Trotterdown. What's this all about?"

"A young woman was murdered about five miles from Trotterdown," Eric said. "On the Landell's Farm."

"And you think I had something to do with it? That's preposterous. I wouldn't harm a fly."

"We don't think anything at the moment," Harriet assured him. "We just need to ask you a few questions, that's all."

Three hours later, Wilde sat opposite Harriet and DI Killian in the interview room. Wilde's lawyer sat next to him. He wasn't too impressed about being dragged away from London at such a late hour. Killian turned on the recording device. "Interview with Graham Wilde commenced 20:45. Present are DI Killian, DC Taylor and Mr Wilde's legal representative, George Harris. Mr Wilde, thank you for your time. We appreciate you coming in."

"I wasn't given much choice," Wilde said. "Can we please get this over with? I have to be back at work tomorrow morning."

"Yes," Harris agreed. "This is all rather inconvenient."

"Mr Wilde," Killian said. "Do you know why you're here?"

"Something to do with the death of a young woman."

"That's right. A French woman – Lauren Moreau. Do you know anybody by that name?"

"Never heard of her."

"Where were you on the morning of last Saturday?"

"I was here," Wilde said. "Well, I was on my way here. I set off from Grubton on Friday and stayed at a campsite half way. I do the same route every year. I like a bit of routine in my life."

"And what time did you set off from the campsite?" Harriet asked.

"Around ten I think."

"Are you sure?"

"Of course, I'm not sure. I think it was around ten."

"We have a witness who claims you'd already left by eight that morning."

"It could have been earlier, I can't remember. I didn't kill that woman."

"Mr Wilde," Killian said. "You have a criminal record, don't you? Sexual assault."

"Misdemeanor," Wilde corrected him. "Sexual misdemeanor. I was given a suspended sentence. It was something over nothing."

Harriet couldn't believe what she was hearing. "Something over nothing? You assaulted a young woman in the ladies toilets."

"DC Taylor," Harris intervened. "My client was handed a lesser sentence. I'd ask you to bear that in mind. My client does not have a sexual assault record."

"Mr Wilde," Harriet carried on regardless. "The woman claimed you assaulted her."

"That's what she reckoned. She made it up. Is that what this is all about? A bit of a drunken altercation in a bar one night and I'm a sexual predator?"

"Mr Wilde," Killian said. "Let's go back to the time you set off from the campsite. Let's say it was slightly earlier. Let's say it was around seven. And let's also say you'd travel around 4 miles per hour. Would that be about right."

"Please do not put words in my client's mouth, Inspector."

"Detective Inspector." Killian looked Wilde in the eyes. "Does that sound about right?"

"I suppose so."

"So that would put you in the vicinity of the Landell Farm between nine and ten that morning."

"Around about."

"Did you see anybody else on the trail that morning?" Harriet asked him.

"Nobody. That's one of the reasons I always come at this time of year – I like the peace and quiet."

"Nobody at all?" Killian said. "Take your time and think back."

"I had the path to myself pretty much until I reached Trotterdown. I took out my phone and took a Selfie of myself standing in front of the sign that marks the end of the trail. I like to do that every year."

Harriet realised that something wasn't right. "Mr Wilde, I seem to recall you telling me and my colleague earlier that you lost your phone somewhere between Grubton and Trotterdown."

Wilde looked at his lawyer and scratched his head. "I could've got it wrong. I could have lost the phone somewhere else."

"Detectives," Harris said. "Forgetting where you lost your phone is not against the law."

"No," Killian said. "But murder is. Your client's answers have been rather vague, and I don't think he's telling us everything."

"I don't know what you're talking about," Wilde said. "I've answered every question you've asked me."

"I agree," Harris said. "And I think this interview has gone on long enough. I assume my client is free to leave."

Killian was silent for a few seconds. "No, I'm not satisfied. And you know very well I am well within my rights as a police detective to hold Mr Wilde for another 24 hours before I decide which way to proceed."

CHAPTER TWENTY SIX

"What did you make of him?" Harriet asked DI Killian in the canteen. Graham Wilde was being held in one of the holding cells – he'd protested of course but Killian had been adamant. He wanted to keep him there for another 24 hours to see what else he could find out about the man.

"He lied about losing his phone," Killian said. "And his memory of the times he set off and arrived are very sketchy. The man's a legal clerk – a good memory is a prerequisite for the job. No, there's something not quite right about Graham Wilde."

"What now then?"

"We'll let him stew overnight and make a start early in the morning. It's been a long day and I for one am looking forward to a hot bath and a warm bed. I'll see you bright and early tomorrow."

* * *

Harriet wasn't tired. Even though it had been a busy day her head was clear. She made tea and booted up her computer.

"Let's see what else we can find out, shall we?" she spoke out loud. She typed 'Trotterdown' into the search bar and pressed Enter. The results were disappointing – there was an article about the women's bowling team right at the top. Apparently, they had qualified to play in a tournament in Germany next year.

"Marvellous."

She tried to narrow down the search and keyed in Trotterdown Echo. She was in luck – the local newspaper had joined the 21st century and now had an online forum. Harriet opened up the page and clicked on the 'archives' link.

"Damn it," the archives only dated back three or four years. "Somebody must know what happened to the German we found in the rocks at Landell's farm."

Harriet finished her tea and made another cup. She sat down in front of the computer once more.

What do we know? She thought. *A man has been lying dead for between fifteen and twenty years. He was wearing a very unique pair of boots that were manufactured by a German company in the mid to late nineties. Jon Finch put his age at around twenty. This wasn't an old tramp who took shelter from the cold and froze to death. This was something else entirely and I'm going to find out what happened to him. Bugger what DS Duncan says.*

The clock at the bottom of the screen read 22:45 and yet Harriet still wasn't tired. Killian had told her they were to make an early start in the morning, but Harriet knew she wouldn't be able to sleep without a bit of help. She remembered the last time she'd taken the pills and they hadn't really worked – she'd woken late and a mist had clogged her mind for the whole of the next morning.

No, not tonight.

"Think," she said. "How do I find out about something that happened twenty years ago?"

She wondered if Jon Finch was still awake. She took out her phone and dialled his number anyway.

Finch answered on the third ring. "Harriet. And here was me thinking insomnia was exclusive to me."

"Good," Harriet said. "You're awake. I need to ask you something."

"Ask away."

"How long have you lived in Trotterdown?"

"Six years. I told you that the other night."

"No, you didn't."

"I did, although you were rather, how can I put it – away with the alcohol fairies."

Harriet couldn't remember much about that night. "I'm never drinking again."

"Why do you ask anyway?"

"I'm still curious about the body we found at Landell's Farm – the man with the unusual boots. Somebody must know how he got there."

"You're becoming obsessed."

"No, I'm not. I can't stop wondering how he got there. Somebody must know something about it."

"Like I said, I've only been here for six years – I moved here from Bristol. I told you that too, but if you're so keen to find out something why don't you ask around? There are plenty of people who've lived their whole lives in this town. DS Duncan for example."

"Duncan has told me in no uncertain terms I'm to leave it well alone. He got rather cross about it."

"Then ask somebody else. In case you haven't noticed, Trotterdown is abuzz with nosy old folk who've spent their whole lives here."

"You're right."

"Just be careful though," Finch warned.

"What harm can it do?"

"I don't know why Duncan is so keen to keep you in the dark, but it would be better if he didn't find out you've gone behind his back and disobeyed an order."

"Duncan doesn't scare me."

"Nor me – all I'm saying is try to be discreet."

"I can do discreet. What does the weather forecast look like for this weekend?"

"Dire. There's no way I'm taking the Albatross out in that. Fifty knot gusters blowing straight from the south-west."

"Sounds perfect."

"You're not right in the head, Harriet Taylor. I have to go – I have an early start in the morning."

"Me too," Harriet said. "Speak soon."

She made a third cup of tea and sat on the sofa in the living room. She was still thinking about the other body. She tried to put it out of her head and think about the Lauren Moreau investigation but something about the discovery of the old corpse had grabbed her attention and it wasn't showing any signs of letting go.

Who was this man? And why is DS Duncan so afraid of me finding out?

CHAPTER TWENTY SEVEN

1996

James Young was worried sick. His daughter, Jane hadn't come home. He'd phoned all her friends and was informed by one of them that Jane had stayed late at school in detention, but she still ought to have been home over an hour ago. James didn't know what to do. He decided to go out and look for her himself. The wind had picked up as he walked from the Unicorn pub in the direction Jane normally walked back from the school. There wasn't a soul on the streets – the weather seemed to have kept everyone indoors. He passed the harbour and carried on along Pier Street. The wind was picking up the water and slamming it onto the jetty below. There was no sign of his daughter. He made his way up the hill towards Jane's school. The school was deserted.

James started to panic – it wasn't like Jane to go off without telling him first. The detention had ended long ago, he'd spoken to all of her friends and none of them knew where she was. He quickened his pace and walked back towards the harbour. He reached Pier Street again and, as he walked past the access road where the wheelie bins stood, he spotted something out of the corner of his eye. There was something on the ground about ten metres into the access road.

Jane Young was frozen stiff, but she was still alive. Her whole body was shaking when her Dad bent down and rested her on his lap. The first thing he did was pull up her school trousers.
"It's alright, princess," he said. "Everything will be alright."
He took off his thick coat and wrapped her up tightly. He lay her down carefully. "I'm going to get some help. I'll be back right away."
"Dad," Jane whispered.

"Don't try to talk. I'm going to fine a phone. I won't let anything happen to you."

He ran to the nearest house and banged on the door. It was opened a few seconds later by an elderly man in a tracksuit.

"I need your help," James said. "My baby girl's been hurt. We need an ambulance."

"What happened?" the man asked.

"I don't know what happened. All I know is she's in a bad way. She's frozen stiff. I need to use your phone."

James returned to his daughter and waited for the ambulance. "There's help on the way. You just hang in there. I'm not going to leave you."

"I wasn't smoking, Dad," Jane rasped. "It was some other girls. I was just standing there."

"I know, baby. It doesn't matter. The ambulance is on the way."

"He came out of nowhere. He had a knife and I screamed."

"Don't try and talk. You're going to be OK. I won't let anything happen to you."

"It was him. It was the same man who tried to attack me by the Landell's Farm."

She coughed, and blood started to pour from her mouth.

The ambulance arrived five minutes later. Two paramedics got out.

"What happened?" the taller of the two asked James.

"My daughter's hurt. That's what bloody happened."

"Let's have a look shall we."

He bent down and had a closer look. He removed James Young's coat and noticed the blood on her school shirt. "OK, let's get you into the ambulance." They managed to get her onto a stretcher and wheeled her inside."

"I'm coming with her," James insisted.

    Jane Young died before they even reached the hospital. The knife wounds were deep, and she'd lost a substantial amount of blood. James watched as all the life drained out of his daughter on that stretcher.

"Do something!" he screamed at one of the paramedics. "Help her."

"She's gone," the paramedic said softly. "She's gone."

CHAPTER TWENTY EIGHT

For once, Harriet was the first to arrive at the station for the scheduled case meeting. George Harris, Graham Wilde's lawyer was standing at the front desk. He appeared to be arguing with the duty officer.

"Is there a problem?" Harriet asked when she reached the desk.

Harris was very red in the face. "You're damn right there's a problem. I want to speak to whoever is in charge of this menagerie."

Harriet looked at the duty officer. He was a man in his late forties who she'd hardly ever spoken to. His name tag read PC Potter.

"Superintendent Lemon isn't in yet," Potter said.

"What's this all about?" Harriet asked Harris.

"You know damn well what it's about. You lock up my client without reason – well my problem is about to become your problem. You can be damn sure of that."

"Sir," Harriet said. "Your client is a suspect in a murder investigation – we are well within our rights to hold him here until we decide otherwise, and I would ask you to kindly watch your language in here. This is a public space and I for one don't appreciate it."

Harris opened his mouth a few times. He resembled a goldfish gasping for air in a tank.

"We have the right to keep Mr Wilde here for at least another 12 hours," Harriet continued. "And then we will decide whether he will be charged or not. You will be kept in the loop at all times. "

DI Killian came in and Harriet breathed a sigh of relief. The decision to hold Graham Wilde had been his, after all – he could deal with the irate lawyer.

"Morning," Killian said cheerily. He looked at PC Potter. "Is everything alright? Is there a problem with Mr Wilde?"

"No problem, sir," Potter said.

"Good. Harriet, we have a lot to get through today and the sooner we start the sooner I can make a decision about Mr Wilde." He nodded to Wilde's lawyer and walked away before George Harris had a chance to say anything.

"You're in a good mood this morning," Harriet said to the DI in his office.

"I had the best night's sleep in weeks. And to top it all off I was treated to breakfast in bed this morning. At first I had to think hard about whether it was my birthday or not."

"You're lucky. Is Megan getting better?"

"Megan's never going to get better, but I've learned to start taking every day as it comes. To start enjoying the good days and today was one of those days. Where's everybody else?"

"I'm sure they'll be in shortly. Have you thought anything more about what to do about Graham Wilde?"

Killian looked at his watch. "We've got a little over 12 hours to play with. I want to dig a bit deeper into his past – see if there's anything else he's been holding back and then I want to interview him again. Maybe a night in the holding cell will have jogged his memory a bit."

Thomas White knocked on the door and walked in with Eric.

"Are we late?" Eric asked.

"Right on time," Killian said. "Take a seat and I'll bring you up to speed on what we've got so far."

The two Whites sat on either side of Harriet.

"OK," Killian began. "This is how we stand at the moment. Graham Wilde spent a night in the holding cell. I'm sure it was rather unpleasant for him and I'm hoping he's going to be more cooperative this morning."

"His lawyer is still lingering," Thomas told him.
"Let him. There's not much he can do. This is the plan. Eric, I want you and Thomas to do a bit of digging around in Mr Wilde's past. Speak to friends, relatives, work colleagues, everybody who knows him. Harriet, I want you to go back to Landell's Farm with Wilde's photograph. Someone working on the farm might recognise him. I hope you're feeling energetic because I need you to walk back along the coast-to coast trail and stop everybody you meet along the way. With any luck you might bump into that woman walking her dog again. Let's get to it then – time is of the essence. I want you all back here at 1 for a briefing before we interview Mr Wilde again."

* * *

Harriet stopped outside the run-down farmhouse and switched off the engine. It was still early morning, but the farm was already a hive of activity. Harriet spotted Donovan Beech in the distance. He was coming towards her on one of the modified quad bikes. He was carrying something on the back. As he got closer, Harriet could see it was a large sheep. He stopped next to her car.
"What do you want?"
"Is Mr Landell here?" Harriet asked him.
"Of course, he is. This is the busiest time of year in case you forgot." Harriet pointed to the sheep in the back of the quad. It didn't appear to be moving. "What's that?"
"It's a bloody Kangaroo – what the hell does it look like? Looks like something got hold of it."
"A fox?"
"A fox couldn't tackle a big one like this. No, I'd say it was dogs. It happens sometimes. What are you doing back here?"

Harriet took out the photograph of Graham Wilde and showed it to him. "Do you recognise this man?"

Donovan Beech studied the photo for a while. "Hmm, his face does seem familiar. Who is he?"

"Have you seen him around here?"

"I know where I've seen him. He does the coast-to-coast trail. Same time each year if I'm not mistaken. What's he done?"

"We're not sure yet."

"Is this about the murder of the French woman?"

"I can't comment on that."

"He's definitely been here before – I seldom forget a face."

"Can you remember the last time you saw him?"

"Recently. I'm not sure exactly where it was but I'm sure it'll come back to me. Do you think he had something do with the woman's death? He looks quite harmless to me."

"Like I said, I can't comment on that."

"He was definitely here recently," Beech said. "Last weekend if I'm not mistaken. Saturday or Sunday."

"Can you remember when it was exactly?"

"It was Saturday. Definitely Saturday. I'd just come back from town and I spotted him on the path. It must have been around nine in the morning – maybe a bit later."

"Are you sure?"

Beech tapped his head. "Like I said, I seldom forget a face."

Harriet thought of something else. "Mr Beech, you've been living here for a while, haven't you?"

"I told you, I was born here. 1968."

"Something happened about twenty years ago. Can you remember a tourist being here around that time? Probably German."

"German? Not off hand. Twenty years is a long time to remember something. A lot of tourists have come and gone in that time."
Harriet didn't want to tell him about what she suspected about the body they'd found in the rocks. She had to tread carefully. "I think something happened to this tourist. He just disappeared."
"Disappeared? He probably just went home to Germany."
He certainly didn't go back to Germany, Harriet thought.
"Is there anybody else who's been working on the farm as long as you?" she asked him.
"I've been here the longest. I was here before young Mr Landell was even born. Why all the interest in a tourist after all these years?"
"I'm just curious. Would you be willing to come in and make a statement?"
"A statement?"
"To the effect that you saw Mr Wilde around the farm on Saturday morning."
"I'm busy."
"When you're not so busy then. We can arrange it when you've finished work."
"I'll see what I can do." He pointed to the dead sheep in the quad. "Now if you don't mind, I have to sort this mess out."

CHAPTER TWENTY NINE

"This isn't looking good for our Mr Wilde," Killian said in his office. Harriet had just told him about Donovan Beech's claim that he saw Wilde on the path near to the farm on Saturday morning.

"Did the Whites come up with anything while they were digging around?" she asked the DI

"Not as yet. But we have enough to charge him."

"Something's bothering me."

"What is it?"

"It's just a feeling I get. Graham Wilde just doesn't strike me as a man who could kill someone in cold blood."

"Harriet, you should know by now that appearances can be deceptive."

"You're probably right – it's just that he's so thin and weakly looking and Lauren Moreau was robust and athletic. Surely she could have fought him off?"

"One blow to the head with a rock is all it takes. Anyway, we're going to charge him with her murder and we'll have a bit more time to play with. We'll need the works from him – DNA sample, fingerprints, hair samples, the lot. And we're going to need his clothes. If there's something that links him to the French woman, Littlemore will find it."

"I'll get onto it. When are we going to interview him again?"

"Soon. Let's see what Eric and Thomas find out and we'll take it from there."

Harriet sat in front of her computer in the office she shared with DS Duncan. Duncan's illness was showing no sign of going away – if anything, it was getting worse. While she waited for the Whites to finish looking into Graham White's past she typed 'Wanderlust' into the address bar. She clicked on Wanderlust's Wikipedia link and scrolled down. The company had been based in Munich and had been run by a man by the name of Rudolph Schweiss. They manufactured high-end outdoor clothing and footwear and closed their doors in 1998. Harriet carried on reading. There were only a few outlets that stocked the Wanderlust range – three in Germany and one in Vienna, Austria. Harriet made a note of all four.

What am I even doing? She thought. *Even if these outlets are still in operation, surely none of them will have kept records from twenty years ago.*

DI Killian came in and Harriet closed the page down.

"My office," the DI sounded quite excited. "Thomas found something interesting."

Harriet sat next to Thomas and Eric in Killian's office. Killian sat opposite them.

"Tell them what you told me," he said to Thomas.

"Looks like we've got our man," Thomas began. "Graham Wilde isn't who he appears to be. I spoke to his sister in Dorset – she hasn't spoken to him in years, and she has good reason."

"What do you mean?" Harriet asked.

"Let him finish," Killian said.

"Our Mr Wilde has a history of depravity," Thomas continued. "If that's the right word. When he was in his first year of senior school he was expelled for hiding out in the girls changing rooms on more than one occasion. Another time he was caught in a tree with a pair of binoculars across the road from a young woman. His sister told me more but I'm sure you get the picture."

Harriet shook her head. "So, the guy's a bit of a perv – a peeping Tom, it doesn't make him a murderer."

"There's more," Thomas said. "I also spoke to his previous employer in Poole. He was dismissed for groping a fellow employee. He held the woman down and indecently assaulted her."

"Why weren't the police involved?" Eric asked.

"The woman was persuaded to keep quiet," Thomas explained. "The company wanted to keep it internal and promised her that if she went no further, Wilde would be dismissed and that would be the end of it."

"That's despicable," Harriet said. "He should have been arrested."

"Yes," Killian agreed. "But that's neither here nor there at the moment. We now know what he's capable of. Littlemore is busy comparing the samples we got from Wilde with the crime scene evidence, so we'll know more then but before we get the results back I want to interview Mr Wilde again. Confront him with this new information and see what he has to say about it."

Graham Wilde was escorted into Interview room 2 by one of the uniformed officers. His solicitor came in with him. Harriet and DI Killian were already seated. The first thing Harriet noticed was how awful Wilde looked. His face was pale, his eyes puffy and bloodshot and his hair sprouted randomly from various places on his head. The night in the holding cell had obviously not agreed with him.

"Mr Wilde," Killian began. "Sleep well?"

Wilde snorted. "What the hell do you think? This is outrageous. You lot are going to pay for this – I happen to know some very influential people in the legal profession."

"I'm sure you do. Let's make a start, shall we?" Killian turned on the recording device. "Interview with Graham Wilde commenced 9:30. Present DI Killian, DC Taylor and Mr Wilde's legal representative, George Harris. Graham, some new information has come to light."

"What new information?" George Harris asked.

"Two pieces of information actually. We know all about the incident at your previous employers."

"That never went any further," Wilde insisted.

"Just like the indecent assault charge that was dropped?" Harriet joined in. "There's a pattern forming here – wouldn't you agree."

Harris glared at her. "Constable, I'd ask you to watch what you say – none of what you have can be used against my client."

"Your client was seen in the vicinity of Landell's farm around the time the young French woman was killed," Killian looked at Wilde. "What have you got to say about that?"

"So, I was there," Wilde said. "That doesn't prove anything."

"No," Harris agreed. "What you have is all circumstantial."

"Your client has lied on tape two or three times," Taylor pointed out. "He was seen at the scene of the murder around the time the woman was killed, he has a history of sexual assault."

"Like I said this is all circumstantial. Unless you provide something concrete you have nothing. I don't have to remind you that time is running out for you." Harris looked at his watch. "The clock is ticking."

Killian left it at that. He knew he had less than 12 hours to come up with some physical evidence against Graham Wilde. After that he would have to let him go.

"What now, sir?" Harriet asked him in the DI's office.

Killian looked at the clock on the wall. "We wait to see what Littlemore can dig up. In the meantime, I want you and Eric to go back to the farm. Sometimes asking the same questions over and over again helps to make people remember. Somebody else might have seen Graham Wilde that day. The more witnesses we have, the stronger the case against the man."

"You're positive it was him, aren't you?"

"Not quite positive but everything points in his direction. He has a history of assaults against women."

"I still can't picture him as a killer."

"Maybe he's been working up to murder. Maybe he got brave this time. Who knows? See what you can find out at the farm."

CHAPTER THIRTY

Landell's Farm was much quieter when Harriet and Eric White got out of the car. The chaos of the past few days appeared to have calmed down. They made their way to the farmhouse. Harriet was about to knock on the door when she heard something inside. It was a woman's voice and she was screaming.

"Someone's getting an ear bashing," Eric had heard it too.

The screams got louder, and a resounding crash could be heard. Harriet knocked on the door and opened it.

"Hello," she shouted. "Police. Is everything alright?"

William Landell Junior appeared in the kitchen doorway. His nose was bleeding and he had a large bruise on his cheek.

"What do you want?" he asked Harriet. "Now really isn't a good time."

"What happened to your face?" Eric asked him.

"Pregnant women are not creatures to be messed with," Landell rubbed his cheek. "We had a bit of a difference of opinion, that's all. What are you doing here?"

"We need to speak to everybody again," Harriet said.

"There's only me, Gilly and Donovan here right now. The lambing chaos has eased off a bit and I've given the other hands a well-deserved rest."

"Then we'll start with the three of you."

"Can we go outside? I want to give Gilly a moment to calm down."

William Landell Junior stood against the wall of the farmhouse, took out a packet of cigarettes and lit one. "I don't normally smoke but the past few weeks have been particularly stressful – more so with the baby on the way and Gilly's hormones. Not to mention the dead body found down by the rocks. What is it you want to know?"

Harriet took out the photograph of Graham Wilde and showed it to Landell. "Do you know this man?"
Landell glanced at the photograph and exhaled a cloud of smoke. "He does seem familiar. Who is he?"
"Have you seen him around here recently?" Eric asked him.
"No. I can't say that I have."
"Are you sure?" Harriet said
"Look, I've got a terrible memory for faces – names too if I'm to be honest. Gilly is more of the memory freak. I don't know how she does it, but she can remember the names of just about everybody she's ever met."
"Then let's show her the photo," Eric suggested.
Landell rubbed the bruise on his cheek again. "If it's alright with you, I'll stay out here and finish my smoke."
    The door to the farmhouse was open. Harriet knocked, and she and Eric went inside. "Mrs Landell, police. Could we have a word?"
The sounds of footsteps could be heard from the creaky stairway and Gilly Landell appeared halfway up. "What's wrong?"
"Nothing to worry about," Harriet told her. "We'd just like you to have a look at a photograph, that's all."
Gilly walked down to them. She held on to the banister tightly. "Where's the photo?"
Harriet held it out to her and Gilly took it and examined it closely.
"I know him. I definitely know that face." She closed her eyes for a few seconds, opened them, and looked at the photograph once more. "He's the creepy hiker. He does the coast-to-coast the same time every year."
"Are you sure?" Eric said.
"I never forget a face."

"Have you seen him around here in the last week or so?" Harriet asked.

"Yes. A few days ago, although it could be more. I was on the quad at the far edge of the farm – where it meets the hiking trail, and I saw him then." Her eyes closed again. "I was checking for walkabouts."

"Walkabouts?" Eric said.

"Some of the ewes like to hit the road once in a while. Especially during the early days of lambing. It was Saturday morning if I can recall."

"Can you remember what time this was?" Harriet asked.

"Early. I'd say around seven."

"And it was definitely him?" Eric added.

"Definitely. I found a rogue ewe that needed bringing back so I didn't pay him any more attention. It was definitely Saturday morning."

"Mrs Landell," Harriet said. "You mentioned something about a creepy hiker. What did you mean by that?"

"Oh, you know – he just has that air about him. There's definitely something not quite right about him."

"Thank you, Mrs Landell. We won't take up any more of your time."

William Landell Junior was talking to Donovan Beech next to a fence fifty metres away from the Farmhouse when Harriet and Eric got back outside. They appeared to be sharing a joke. Beech's hearty guffaw could be heard from the house. Harriet and Eric walked up to them. The laughing stopped when Beech spotted them.

"What are you doing back here?" he addressed his question to Harriet.

"Mr Beech, when I showed you the photograph of the coast-to-coast hiker earlier you told me he was around the farm at around nine on Saturday morning."

"Did I?"

"Yes, you did. Are you absolutely sure it was that time?"
Gilly Landell had put him there two hours earlier.
"It was around nine, maybe later. I'd gone into town and he was hanging around when I got back. Definitely after nine."

"What exactly is going on here?" Landell asked. "Why the sudden interest in this hiker? Do you think he had something to do with the murder of that French girl?"
"We don't think anything at the moment," Harriet said. "We're just following up on a few things. I'll let you get back to work."

CHAPTER THIRTY ONE

1996

James Young stood with his head bowed outside the small church in Trotterdown. William and Lily Landell stood by his side. Lily had her hand on James' back. James had just buried his only daughter, Jane. "I don't know how I'm ever going to get over this," he said. "Jane was my life – she was the reason I did everything I did. And now she's gone."
"We're all sorry, love," Lily Landell said. "I can't imagine what you're going through but if you need anything, you just have to ask."
"That's right," Lily's husband agreed. "Anything you need."
"Right now, I need a drink and then I'm going to do everything I can to find out what happened to my baby girl. Whoever did this is going to pay, you mark my words. Can you leave me now? I want to spend some time with Jane on my own."

He made his way towards the freshly dug grave in the small churchyard and shivered as he read the headstone above where his daughter was buried. "Trotterdown was supposed to be a fresh start for us, love," he spoke quietly. "Away from the bad elements in London. I let you down but I'm going to make it right. I promise you, I'm going to make it right if it's the last thing I ever do."
He moved one of the flowers in the cemetery vase, so it was in line with the others and walked away from the churchyard.

* * *

The Unicorn was packed to the brim. In the short time James Young had been in Trotterdown, he had proven to be a very popular landlord and most of the town had turned up to show their respects.

William Landell was sitting at the bar with Pete, one of James Young's poker playing friends.

"How are you holding up, James?" Pete asked him. "Can we get you anything?"

"I need a strong one," James replied. "And then I need a quiet word."

"Double scotch," Pete asked the barman. "Make that two."

They took their drinks outside to the small beer garden.

"I'm so sorry, mate," Pete said. "What is it you want to talk to me about?"

"What do you think? You're the copper. I want to know what's happening in the investigation into my baby girl's death."

"You know I can't tell you much there."

"I've just buried my princess – doesn't that mean anything?"

"Of course it does."

"Then what have you got. Some bastard killed my girl. Have you spoken to the Austrian upstart again?"

"He's gone. Disappeared into thin air. Nobody's seen him for days."

"What did you find at the scene? What have forensics got to go on?"

"Like I said, I can't go into that." He downed the whisky in his glass. "We'd better get back inside."

"I'm going to get to the bottom of this if it's the last thing I do."

"Just let us do our job. I know you're angry right now, but you won't do yourself any favours digging around and getting in our way."

James Young looked Pete in the eye. "I'll do whatever it takes and nobody – including you, had better stand in my way."

CHAPTER THIRTY TWO

"We've got two conflicting sightings of Graham Wilde on Saturday morning," Harriet told DI Killian in his office. "Gilly Landell claims she saw him there at around seven and Donovan Beech reckons he was there two hours later."

"Who do you believe?" Killian asked.

"I don't know. They both seemed quite certain."

"I don't think it really matters anyway. Two people can put him by the farm on Saturday morning. That's enough for me." Killian glanced at his watch. "We've only got a few hours left before we have to charge him or let him go."

"What are we going to do?"

"Charge him with the murder of Lauren Moreau. He's lied to us on more than one occasion – he has a history of sexual assault and he was seen at the scene of the crime by at least two people. That's enough for me. Let's have another crack at him and see if he feels like telling us what really happened."

Harriet still had doubts. Something didn't feel right. She didn't like Graham Wilde one little bit, but that did not make him a murderer. Killian was busy getting the ball rolling with the prosecutor in Plymouth, George Harris, Wilde's legal adviser had been informed and Graham Wilde himself was waiting in the cells to find out what was going to happen to him. The evidence against him was all circumstantial and Harriet knew it would take quite a bit of persuading to convince the crown prosecutor to formally charge a man with murder when all they had was a couple of witness statements and a history of sexual assault. They needed hard evidence.

From the smile on Killian's face when he walked in the canteen, Harriet knew the DI had managed to talk the prosecutor round. Killian sat down opposite her. "We've got another 48 hours. The CPS don't think we've got enough on Wilde to formally charge him, but they do agree that the evidence we do have warrants another two days to gather as much as we can."

"Has Mr Wilde been informed?" Harriet asked.

"He has. And he's not too pleased about it."

"I bet he isn't. Are we going to interview him again?"

"Not yet. I've spoken to Littlemore and he's just about finished in forensics. We've got an extra two days to link Graham Wilde to the scene of the crime. That is our main priority right now. It's getting late, so I suggest we crack on first thing in the morning. At least we know that Mr Wilde isn't going anywhere in the meantime. Let's see what forensics can come up with and take it from there. I want everybody back here at six thirty."

* * *

Harriet drove home the long way. She stopped her car at the top of Merryhead and got out. The ocean was calmer than she's seen it in a very long time. The weather front Jon Finch had warned her about was obviously still quite a way off. Harriet breathed in the sea breeze and closed her eyes. Her mind felt clear. She thought about the Lauren Moreau murder – there was something they were missing. And it was something important. Graham Wilde just didn't fit as a murderer. Harriet wasn't sure why – it was something deep in her gut that told her they were looking in the wrong direction. Her thoughts turned to the other body they'd found in the rocks by the farm. That one seemed to have captured her attention much more than the recent one and she was determined to get to the bottom of it.

A corpse is discovered after all this time, she thought. *It's been there for years.*

Harriet opened her eyes and gazed out to sea. Her phone started to ring in her pocket. She answered it.

"Harriet," it was Jon Finch.

"Jon. I was just thinking about you. I thought you said there was a front on the way. I'm up on Merryhead and the ocean's like a pond."

"You'll see. Just wait until tomorrow. All hell's going to break loose. What are you doing at Merryhead?"

"Thinking. Thinking about the man's body we pulled out of the rocks by Landell's Farm. I need to find out who he was and how he got there."

Finch started to laugh. "Harriet Taylor, you have to be the most stubborn person I've ever met. What are you up to this evening?"

"Research," Harriet replied without thinking. "And I'd better get an early night. The DI wants us there early tomorrow – he's persuaded the prosecutor to let us keep Graham Wilde for another 48 hours."

"What about the weekend?"

"Until this investigation is cleared up, there'll be no weekend. You know what it's like?"

"I certainly do. I'll speak to you soon."

Harriet put her phone back in her pocket and walked back to her car. The wind had picked up slightly, and there was a sudden chill in the air. Finch's weather prediction was starting to look more accurate.

When Harriet got of the car outside her house she was almost knocked over by a gust of wind. She hurried inside and headed straight for the kitchen to make some tea. She remembered she'd left a few windows open upstairs so she went up to close them while the kettle boiled. She made the tea and booted up her computer. She glanced through her internet history and found the Wanderlust outdoor clothing company again. There was no website for the company – Harriet knew that very few businesses had websites in those days, but there was a link to the company history that Harriet had overlooked the last time she looked.

"Wanderlust, Freiburg," she said out loud. "Now this is interesting."

She scrolled down the page. The company started trading in 1992 and closed down six years later. There was a list of the directors of the company. That list numbered two – Rudolph Schweiss and Fritz Weidmuller. Harriet wrote both their names down on the notepad on her desk, closed down the page she was looking at and typed 'Markus Wepener' in the search bar. There were over 350 results. She added the word 'Wanderlust' to the search and narrowed it down to ten. She clicked on the first one. Rudolph Schweiss had opened Wanderlust in August 1992 from his garage. Rudolph was a keen mountaineer and decided there was a gap in the market for superior quality outdoor clothing and footwear. The company had closed six years later for reasons not mentioned on the page. Harried carried on reading to the end. Rudolph Schweiss had been killed during an expedition in the Andes in 2011. She rubbed her eyes and read further. Something halfway down the page caught her eye. It was something Thomas had failed to mention when they first started looking into the Wanderlust range of hiking boots. The boots found on the dead man were from the Wanderlust Mark 4 range. That particular model was only manufactured in 1996.

1996, Harriet thought, *that's twenty-one years ago.*

She finished her tea and made another cup. She sat back down at the computer and typed in 'Fritz Weidmuller'. The first ten entries showed the same man. Weidmuller was an Austrian millionaire who had made his fortune on the stock exchange. As Harriet delved deeper she soon discovered that Weidmuller was merely an investor in Wanderlust. Also, a keen mountaineer, Weidmuller had provided the capital for the business right up until it closed in 1998. Harriet clicked on the second link in the list and discovered that Fritz Weidmuller was still alive and now living in Salzburg.

She carried on reading. Fritz Weidmuller was sixty-five years old. He'd passed on his investment business to his youngest son, Alex and was now retired. There was a telephone number for his firm of investment bankers in Vienna. Harriet wrote it down on her notepad and made a mental note to get in touch with them the following morning. She knew there would be nobody there to answer the phone at this late hour.

Harriet finished her tea and shut down the computer. The wind was now howling outside the living room window, and the temperature inside the house had dropped quite drastically.

A warm bath and good night's sleep, she thought. *That's exactly what I need.*

CHAPTER THIRTY THREE

The wind was blowing so hard when Harriet woke to her alarm clock, it was rattling the windows in her bedroom. She shivered, turned off the alarm and got out of bed. She opened the curtains, looked out the window and saw that the trees in her back garden were straining under the force of the gale. They were bending so much that Harriet was worried they would snap in half. Jon Finch had been spot on – there was no way they could take the boat out in that. She washed her face and brushed her teeth and went downstairs. She made tea and took it through to the living room. She glanced at the notebook next to her computer and remembered the investment company she'd looked up the previous night. She decided she would get hold of them as soon as she had a chance. It was a long shot, but they might be able to give her some kind of idea where the unusual boots found on the corpse under the rocks by Landell's Farm came from. She finished her tea, picked up her car keys and a warm coat and left the house.

The roads were empty as she drove the familiar route to the station in Trotterdown. It was not yet six in the morning and the weather seemed to be playing a part in keeping people indoors. Harriet had to drive slowly the whole way – the wind kept pushing her to the side. She was glad when she'd parked in the car park at the station and made it inside safely.

Eric White was manning the front desk. "How's that weather this morning. They reckon it's only going to get worse – there's rain in buckets on the way."

"Is the DI in yet?" Harriet asked him.

"Not yet. Duncan's here though. He arrived about five minutes before you."

Harriet was surprised. DS Duncan had hardly showed his face at work for the past week or so. "Is he feeling better?"

"Must be."

"I'm going to grab a cup of tea before the meeting this morning."

DS Duncan was sitting by himself in the canteen. He was looking at something on his mobile phone and didn't even notice when Harriet sat down opposite him.

"Morning, sarge," she said. "You're looking much better this morning."

Duncan switched his phone off. "I'm feeling much better – that new pharmacist in town gave me some tonic to try out and it's cleared everything up. I can think straight for the first time in days. I believe there's a briefing at 6:30, do you want to fill me in on what I've missed over the past week?"

Harriet gave him a brief outline of what they had so far. When she'd finished, DS Duncan sighed and then nodded his head.

"Do you reckon this Graham Wilde bloke did it?"

"I don't know," Harriet admitted. "He was definitely there at the time the French woman disappeared and he has a history of sexual deviancy but there's something not quite right about the whole thing."

"What about forensics? Did Littlemore find anything?"

"We'll find out this morning. Part of me hopes he found something to link Wilde to the French girl."

"But..."

"Another part of me knows deep down it wasn't him and I'll be damned if I can figure out why I know this."

"That's what I like to see," Killian walked in. "Bright and early." He looked at DS Duncan. "How are you feeling? I must say your face has a lot more colour in it than the last time I saw you."

"I'm almost 100 percent, Jack," Duncan said. "What's the plan?"

"Littlemore is coming in personally to tell us what he found and from past experience that usually means good news."

"What time is he getting here?" Harriet asked.

"He'll be here before seven. Thomas White is having car troubles, but Eric has gone to fetch him. We'll have a brief meeting in here when they all arrive to go over everything once more, and then you and I are going to have another crack at our Mr Wilde. Hopefully, we'll be armed with something we can use to make him tell us the truth."

Alan Littlemore came in with Eric and Thomas White in tow. They joined Harriet, Duncan and DI Killian at the table.

"What a bloody awful day," Thomas said. "Not the best day for a car to break down."

"What's wrong with it?" Duncan asked him.

"Radiator overheated. Can you believe it – on a day like this? You're looking much better, sarge."

"Right," Killian butted in. "Seeing as we're all here, let's make a start. Alan, please tell us you've found something."

The head of forensics opened up a file, ran his forefinger down the first page and looked the DI in the eyes. "I've got good news and bad news, Jack. Which one would you prefer first?"

"Let's start with the good news," Killian said. "We can worry about the bad news later."

"We re-examined the contents of Lauren Moreau's rucksack. There was a raincoat in there that we didn't pay much attention to earlier. Anyway, we went over it with a fine-toothed comb and found some samples of hair that definitely didn't belong to our dead French woman. The hairs were grey."

"Graham Wilde has traces of grey in his hair," Eric pointed out.

"Let me finish," Littlemore said. "And this brings me to the bad news. We have everything we need from Graham Wilde – fingerprints, DNA and samples of his hair. The grey hair we found on the raincoat did not come from the man waiting in the holding cells."

"Are you sure?" Thomas asked and received a glare from Littlemore by way of a reply.

"Where does that leave us?" Harriet asked. "Didn't you find anything at all to link Graham Wilde to the dead woman?"

"Nothing," Littlemore replied. "There is nothing to indicate that Mr Wilde had any contact with Lauren Moreau whatsoever."

"He was seen by at least two people by the farm at the time we believe Miss Moreau was attacked," Thomas said. "He's a known pervert."

"Be that as it may," Killian said. "You know as well as the rest of us that's not enough to charge him."

"The hairs," Harriet said. "The grey hairs. Were there many of them?"

"Quite a few," Littlemore replied.

"How do you think they got there?"

"What do you mean?"

"Could they have got there by just brushing up against someone in a crowded place? Or if she left the raincoat on the back of a chair? It's not really something we can use anyway, is it?"

"No," the head of forensics glanced at the report again. "The raincoat had Velcro on the sleeves and where the hood is stored. There's more Velcro over the zip. The hairs were all over the Velcro. We also found large traces of what appears to be lanolin on the raincoat. My team are confirming it as we speak but I'm 99 percent sure it's lanolin."

"Lanolin?" Eric White repeated. "Where did that come from?"

"Sheep," Harriet said.

Littlemore grinned at her. "Exactly. And if I were a detective, I'd get back down to Landell's Farm and start asking some more questions."

CHAPTER THIRTY FOUR

"How do you think her jacket got covered in lanolin?" Eric asked Harriet as they made their way once more to Landell's Farm.
"If I remember correctly, lanolin is a fat found in the wool from a sheep," Harriet replied. "She must have come in contact with the sheep at some time."
"Who's got the task of telling Graham Wilde he's free to go?"
"The DI offered to do it. I don't envy him. I doubt Mr Wilde will come back here in a hurry."
She parked outside the farm house next to one of the modified quad bikes. William Landell Junior was standing outside struggling to light a cigarette.

The wind was still howling as Harriet and Eric walked up to him. The bruise on his cheek was now a dark blue colour.
"Morning," Harriet said. "What a horrible day. It's forecast to last the whole weekend."
Landell had managed to light the cigarette and exhaled a huge cloud of smoke. "I know. I've just spent most of the night herding the lambs into the shed – exposure to this can kill them at their age. What are you doing back here? Has the coast-to-coast bloke confessed?"
"I'm afraid not," Harriet told him. "We had to release him – some new evidence has come to light and we couldn't hold him any longer."
"What new evidence?"
"Where are the rest of the farm workers?" Harriet dodged his question.
"Still sorting out the lambs. What exactly is going on here?"

Harriet looked closely at the man standing in front of her. She paid special attention to his hair which was black and turning grey in places. "I'm afraid we're going to need samples of hair from everybody who was working on the farm last Saturday. I assume with the moving of the lambs, they're all here now?"

"That's right. What's this about hair samples? What new evidence have you found?"

"That's not important," Eric said. "Our forensics officer will be along shortly. Like my colleague said, we'll need hair samples from everybody here – including yourself."

William Landell Junior opened his mouth as if to say something but stopped abruptly when his wife, Gilly appeared in the doorway.

"What are they doing back here?" Gilly nodded towards Harriet and Eric.

"They just need to ask a few more questions," Landell told her. "Just routine."

Harriet thought this a strange thing to say – she and Eric hadn't mentioned anything about any further questioning.

"Get yourself inside, love," Landell said to his wife. "You'll catch your death in this gale. You need to look after that little thing inside you."

"So, all of a sudden you give a damn about me and the baby." She looked at Harriet. "Don't let him fool you, detective. I can see straight through this concerned act. He's a bastard – his father before him was a bastard and..."

"Gilly," Landell raised his voice. "Gilly, please stop it and go back inside. I'll sort this out."

Gilly shook her head, went back inside the house and slammed the door behind her.

"It's the hormones," Landell said. "She's not normally like this. She's having a bit of a rough time of it at the moment."

"What's going on here, Mr Landell?" Harriet asked. "Is there something you want to tell us?"

Landell took out another cigarette, turned into the wind and cupped his hand in front of his face to light it. "I knew the French girl. I knew Lauren Moreau."

"Why didn't you tell us this before?" Harriet said.

"I couldn't. I just couldn't. What with Gilly and the baby and everything else that's been going on around here, I couldn't let anyone find out."

"Were you and Lauren sleeping together?" Eric came straight out with it.

Landell bowed his head. "It just happened. Gilly was taking strain with the pregnancy and I was being neglected, if you understand what I mean. I met Lauren for the first time about a year ago. She was here without that arrogant boyfriend of hers and we just seemed to hit it off. It wasn't supposed to be serious, but you know how these things can just happen."

Harriet knew all too well how these things can just happen. She was once married to a man who seemed to let these things happen quite often.

"I didn't kill her," Landell said. "You have to believe me."

"When was the last time you saw Miss Moreau?" Eric asked him.

"Friday evening. She phoned me the day before and told me her and her boyfriend would be at the Backpackers and suggested we meet up."

"And where did this rendezvous take place?" Harriet said.

"There's a secluded spot at the far side of the farm. A cluster of trees that aren't visible from the path."

"The path?"

"The coast-to-coast trail. It's about half a mile away from Trotterdown. Not many people know about it. Gilly wasn't feeling too well so I suggested she should have a lie down for a few hours."
"While you set off to meet your young mistress."
Landell lit another cigarette and sighed. "It wasn't like that. Lauren was already there when I arrived. I went there on one of the quads."
"Then what happened?"
"What do you think happened? We hadn't seen each other for a while. Use your imagination. We stayed there for a couple of hours. Lauren spread her coat out in the back of the quad and we just lay there talking and holding each other."
"The raincoat?" Harriet said.
"What about it?" Landell said.
"You use the quads to transport the sheep, don't you?"
"I modified them a few years back – I had cages made for the sheep. What's that got to do with anything?"

Harriet watched as Alan Littlemore's car drove up the road towards them and parked behind her own car. The head of forensics and DS Duncan got out.
Duncan pulled the collar of his coat around his neck as they approached. "This weather isn't going to do my cold any good. They reckon it's going to bucket it down this afternoon."
"Are we all set?" Littlemore asked Harriet.
"Everyone's here," she replied. "So, we can make a start. Some new information has come to our attention. Can I have a word?"

Littlemore followed her away from the house. They stopped a few hundred metres away.
"What's this new information?" the head of forensics asked.
Harriet told him what William Landell Junior had just confessed to.

"For God's sake," Littlemore said. "Why's he only telling us this now?"

"I suppose he didn't think it would come out. They all think that, don't they?"

"What?"

"Nothing. But I reckon there's a good chance that the hairs on Lauren Moreau's jacket will match those from the philandering farmer over there."

"And the lanolin on the coat is no doubt from the modified quad bike. If Landell uses it to transport sheep it will be covered in the stuff."

"What do you suggest we do now?"

"Collect the hair samples regardless. We still need to find out for sure if they came from Landell. Once it's confirmed, let's see how Killian wants to proceed. Why can't people just tell the truth in the first place? It would make all our jobs a hell of a lot easier."

Harriet was stunned. She'd never known Littlemore to talk like that before.

"Forgive me," he said. "I didn't sleep much last night. How many of them are there to collect samples from?"

"Four – there's Landell and his wife, Donovan Beech and the temp, Tommy Dunn."

"Let's round them up then."

CHAPTER THIRTY FIVE

It took Alan Littlemore less than an hour to determine that the hairs found on Lauren Moreau's coat came from William Landell Junior. Another hour of checking out the other hair samples taken from everyone on the farm and the head of forensics was satisfied that the only hair on the coat came from Landell. DI Killian sat in his office staring at the phone on his desk after taking the call from Littlemore. He left the office and made his way to the canteen. Harriet, DS Duncan and the two Whites were waiting for the results to come through.

"Well?" Duncan asked Killian.

"The hairs were Landell's," the DI told him. "No doubt about it."

"Let's bring him in then," Eric White said.

"I agree," Thomas said. "He's hiding something."

"I don't think he is," Harriet said. "I think he only didn't tell us about the affair because he was afraid of how his wife would react."

"He's a cheater and a liar," Eric said. "Who's to say he's not a murderer too?"

"You're forgetting something, Eric," Harriet said. "William Landell Junior has admitted he was having a relationship with Lauren Moreau. They met on Friday evening. He also admitted they had sex and they lay in the back of the quad for a few hours. There's nothing to suggest he had any reason to kill her. Where's the motive?"

"Maybe she threatened to tell his wife," Thomas suggested. "It's pretty clear he's terrified of his wife."

"No, I still don't buy it."

DI Killian coughed. "We'll bring him in anyway. If Harriet's right, we need to rule him out and start moving in another direction."

"What direction, Jack?" Duncan said. "The Frenchman was a dead end, as was that Graham Wilde pervert. Once Landell Junior's been ruled out, where do you suggest we look?"

"We need to stay positive," Killian said. "Eric, you and Thomas can bring Landell in for questioning. Try to be subtle about it – I realise he's been cheating on his wife, but it'll do this investigation no good at all if we have a rabid Harpy to contend with too."

While Harriet was waiting for the Whites to return with Landell Junior, she switched on her computer and checked her emails. There was nothing new. She remembered something she needed to check. She took out her notebook and turned to the page with the phone number of the Weidmuller Investment Company in Vienna. She dialled the number and waited. It was answered immediately by a woman who spoke German with a husky voice. Harriet didn't know a single word of German.

"Good morning," she said. "I'm sorry but I don't speak German."

"How can I help you?" the woman asked in English.

"My name is Harriet Taylor. I'm a detective constable with the Trotterdown police in Cornwall. I need some information about a company that operated in the 1990's – a company by the name of Wanderlust."

"Wanderlust?" the woman repeated.

"That's right. I believe Mr Weidmuller was the main investor in the company."

"1990's you say?"

"That's right."

"Mr Weidmuller would have been a young boy in the 1990's. Oh you must mean Alex's father, Fritz. I'm afraid he is now retired. He handed the reins over to Alex two years ago."

"Would it be possible for me to speak to Alex?"
"He's away on business in Prague. May I ask what this is all about?"
Harriet realised how ridiculous it would sound if she told the woman that an old corpse was found wearing a pair of boots sold by a company a millionaire financed in the 1990's. "When is Alex Weidmuller due back?"
"Monday morning."
"I'll try again then. Thank you so much for your help."

What was I thinking? Harriet thought after she'd put down the phone. *That poor woman must have thought I was an idiot.*
DS Duncan came in. They shared the office, but Duncan very rarely used it. "What's up?" he asked. "You look like you've been caught with your hand in the sweet jar."
"I feel like such a fool. I just phoned a multi-million Euro investment company to find out some information about a small business its founder put money into almost 20 years ago."
"You've lost me there."
"The other body we found at Landell's Farm. I'm determined to find out who he was. The boots he was wearing are our only lead. It's a long shot, but if I can find out more about the company that sold the boots, maybe we can get a bit closer to finding out who this mystery man is."
"Leave it, Harriet," Duncan raised his voice. "That one's a dead end. Dead end. Have you got that?"
"But, sarge?"
"But, sarge nothing. Can't you get it into your thick, stubborn, Scottish head that some things are better left alone?"
"What are you talking about?"
Harriet was shocked at the words the DS had used.

"What I mean is," Duncan's tone softened. "Is you'll drive yourself crazy obsessing over something that you'll never get to the bottom of. I've been there, done that, got the T-Shirt and I don't want you to go through the same thing. Like I said, some things are better left dead and buried. Let's go and see if the White's have managed to bring Landell in, shall we?"

William Landell Junior sat upright in the chair in Interview Room 1. When Harriet walked in with DI Killian, something struck her immediately – Landell didn't appear to be too worried about being in a police interview room about to be questioned about a murder, his facial expression and body language spoke of something else entirely. Harriet was sure he seemed relieved somehow. Relieved to be able to speak about something that he'd kept inside for too long. Harriet took the seat next to the DI across the table from Landell.

Killian turned on the recording device. "Interview with William Landell commenced 12:25. Present DI Killian and DC Taylor. For the record, Mr Landell has declined the offer of legal representation. Mr Landell, do you understand why you're here today?"

Landell nodded. "I do. I didn't kill Lauren Moreau."

"Mr Landell, could you please tell us what your relationship was with Miss Moreau?"

"I met Lauren about a year ago. I first saw her at the Unicorn. It was in March or April I think. She was on her own and she walked in and sat a chair away from me at the bar. The pub was quiet, and we soon got talking. I liked her. We hit it off straight away."

"Go on."

"I was having trouble at home. Gilly was giving me hell about not being able to give her a child."

"For the record, Gilly is your wife, isn't she?"

"That's right. My home life was hell and so I tried to get out as much as I could. Lauren was a welcome distraction from all that."

"Did you have a sexual relationship with Miss Moreau?" Harriet asked him.

"Yes," Landell said straight away. "Lauren was like nothing I'd ever seen before. She was a free spirit and I suppose that's one of the reasons I fell for her – she was the total opposite of Gilly. We've been seeing each other on and off since last year. Whenever Lauren had a chance, she'd come over and we'd meet up."

"When did you last see Miss Moreau?" Killian asked.

"Friday evening. I got a call from her on Thursday to let me know she'd be in the area for a week or so and we arranged to meet up. I took the quad and met her at a private spot about half a mile from Trotterdown."

"And what happened there?" Harriet said.

"Do you want me to spell it out?"

"No," Killian butted in. "I don't think that's necessary. And are you sure that was the last time you saw her?"

"Positive. I couldn't get away after that – what with the lambing and everything. I didn't kill her."

"Can you think of anybody who might have wanted to hurt Miss Moreau?" Harriet said.

Landell looked at his watch. "Of course not. She was a beautiful, spirited young lady. I can't imagine anybody wanting to kill her."

"Do you still have the record of the phone call on Thursday?" Harriet asked.

"Excuse me?"

"You said she phoned you on Thursday and asked if you'd like to meet. I assume her phone call is still recorded on your phone."

Landell took out his mobile phone and put it on the table.
Harriet picked it up. "Do you mind if I have a look?"
"Go ahead. I've already told you, I didn't kill her. I've got nothing to hide."

Harriet opened up the call history for Thursday. Landell had received six calls that day. Five were from his wife, Gilly and the other was a number he'd saved on his phone under the initials LM.
"Is this her?" Harriet pointed to the number. "She phoned you at 6:30."
"That's it."

Harriet continued looking through the list of phone calls Landell had received after Lauren Moreau had phoned. Then she checked the message history. One of them caught her eye. "Mr Landell, you told us earlier that the last you heard from Miss Moreau was on Friday evening. Is that right?"
"That's right."
"And you weren't in contact with her at all after that evening?"
"No. What are you getting at?"
"Are you sure? You didn't phone her or send her any messages?"
"Of course, I'm sure."
"A message was sent from this phone to Miss Moreau at 7:30 on Saturday morning. 'Meet you at the usual place at 8'."
"I didn't send any messages."
"And a reply was received 2 minutes later. 'See you there. X.'"

CHAPTER THIRTY SIX

"He reckons he didn't send the message," Killian finished filling in DS Duncan and the Whites about what had transpired in the interview.
"And do you believe him?" Duncan asked.
"He seemed genuinely shocked," Harriet said.
"He's cheated on his wife," Eric White pointed out. "You don't get away with something like that without being a bit of a devious bastard." Harriet was inclined to agree – her husband had got away with his two-timing for the duration of their marriage. To be able to have an affair undetected required a certain amount of conniving.
Killian ran his hands through his hair. "Let's go through the chain of events once more. Lauren Moreau's body was discovered on Sunday morning by Gilly Landell. The path reports show she'd been buried by the rocks for roughly 24 hours. Plus, we have William Landell Junior's statement to testify she was with him on Friday evening. Her boyfriend claims she set off on the coast-to-coast at around 7 on Saturday. That gives us a window of around an hour and a half. The message was sent from Landell's phone at 7:30 on Saturday. If they met at 8 as suggested by the message, I'd say it's safe to assume whoever sent that message killed her."
"Are you saying you don't think Landell sent the message, sir?" Eric said.
"I'm just looking at the facts. Does anybody have anything to add?"

"Motive," Harriet said after a few seconds had passed. "Landell Junior doesn't appear to have any reason to have wanted Lauren Moreau dead. From what I can gather, their relationship was hardly based on anything more than a quick romp in the hay. I don't believe

Lauren wanted anything more than that, so she'd have no reason to want to spill the beans to Landell's wife."

"A woman scorned is a dangerous thing," Thomas said.

"But Lauren wasn't the one who was being scorned," Harriet pointed out. "Gilly Landell was. Unless…"

"Unless what?" Eric said. "I hate it when you do that."

"It's just a possible scenario," Harriet said. "What if Gilly Landell knew about the affair? What if she's known about it all along? How do you think that made her feel – especially now there's a child on the way? She would have access to her husband's mobile phone. She sends Lauren a message pretending to be William suggesting they meet at 8. Lauren replies, and the meeting takes place. Only it's Gilly who turns up and not William – she kills Lauren, buries her and waits a day to conveniently find the body. All she needs to do then is wait."

"This is a bit far-fetched isn't it?" Duncan said.

"No, it's not. The more you think about it, the more it makes sense. Who would suspect a pregnant woman?"

"Why did she leave the message on the phone?" Thomas said. "Surely, if she did kill Lauren Moreau, it would be risky to leave the message. Her husband could quite easily have seen it."

"Unless…" Harriet said.

"You're doing it again, Harriet," Eric pointed out.

"Sorry. Maybe Gilly Landell left the message on William's phone to implicate her husband. It's a perfect plan. All you need is a basic understanding of police procedure – you can get that from any detective show on TV, we always check phone records. We find the message, the timeline fits, and William Landell Junior is suddenly our number one suspect."

Harriet hadn't noticed that a smile had formed on Killian's face as he listened to her hypothesis.

"OK," the DI said. "Harriet, you have some valid points there, but we have to tread very carefully. Firstly, if Gilly Landell did mastermind all of this we mustn't underestimate her. And secondly, if we're wrong you can imagine how this is going to look."

"Dragging a poor pregnant woman in to interrogate her," Eric said. "Old Lemon will have a hernia."

"Where is the superintendent these days?" Thomas asked.

"He's around," Killian said. "Eric's right. If we make a balls-up of this, the press will be all over us like a rash."

"What do we do then?" Harriet asked.

"We work on her husband first."

"What do you mean?" Eric asked.

"We'll interview Landell again, and imply we're going to bring his wife in regarding the messages on his phone. Either he's telling the truth and he didn't send the message or he's the one that sent it. Either way, I've got a feeling that once he realises his wife is going to find out about the affair, he might become a bit more pliable and give us something to go on. I'm also going for a change of dynamic. Pete, are you up to interviewing him?"

DS Duncan smiled. "You and me, Jack? It'll be like the old days. Let's have a crack at him."

* * *

William Landell Junior sat down once again on a chair in Interview 1. DS Duncan and Killian sat opposite him. Killian started the recording device.

"Second interview with William Landell Junior commenced 14:30. Present DI Killian and DS Duncan. William, how are you feeling?"

"Numb," Landell replied. "I can't believe all this is happening. I didn't kill Lauren. I've already told you that."

"OK," Killian said softly. "Let's go back to what we spoke of earlier. Your phone records."

Landell's phone had been taken into evidence.

"You admitted to receiving a phone call from Lauren Moreau at..." He opened up a file in front of him. "6:30 that evening. Is that correct?"

"That's right," Landell said.

Killian ran his finger down the paper in the file. "And the next morning at 7:30 a text message was sent from your phone to Miss Moreau's number. For the record I will read what was said in that message – 'Meet you at the usual place at 8'. Two minutes later a reply came through 'See you there. X.'"

"I didn't send that message," Landell insisted. "I know nothing about the texts on my phone."

"So you said. How did they get there then?"

"I have no idea."

"Mr Landell," DS Duncan joined in. "This isn't looking good for you. A text is sent from your phone asking to meet a young woman at the usual place. An hour or so later, this woman is attacked and left for dead. Where exactly is this 'usual place'?"

Landell was now starting to show signs of stress. Beads of sweat were appearing on his forehead. "There's a secluded spot on the edge of the farm where we'd meet up. It's pretty hidden from the path and the farm."

"And not too far from where Miss Moreau's body was found," Killian pointed out.

"This really isn't looking good for you, William," Duncan added.

"OK," Killian continued. "William, I'm going to ask you again. How did that text message end up on your phone?"

"I really don't know."

"Who else has access to the phone?"

"Nobody. What time was the message sent again?"

"7:30 in the morning," Duncan reminded him.

Landell scratched his head and something changed in his facial expression. It was as if he'd come to some kind of realisation. "I keep my phone in my jacket pocket most of the time but at half-seven in the morning it was probably lying on the kitchen table."

"Go on," Duncan urged.

"The only person who would be able to send a message would have been Gilly."

"That's what we thought," Killian came out with it at last.

"But..." Landell's eyes opened wider. "No, this can't be right. Why would Gilly send Lauren a text from my phone asking to meet at our usual place?"

"That's what we're trying to ascertain, William," Duncan said. "How long have I known you?"

"Since I was a boy."

"You've always been a hardworking man – your old man would've been proud, you've never been in trouble with the law, but this isn't looking good for you. Is there anything else you want to tell us?"

Landell's brow furrowed as though he was finding it hard to think. "Do you think Gilly knew about the affair? How could she? I always made sure I covered my back and... And if she did know and it was her who sent that massage from my phone. Surely you can't think..."

"Think what, William?" Killian asked him.

"Gilly has a temper on her but, murder? No, I don't believe it."

"I think we can take a short break there," Killian suggested. "Interview with William Landell Junior paused 14:55." He pressed stop on the machine. "William, I'll arrange for a cup of tea to be brought in. Is there anything else I can get for you?"

Landell cupped his face in his hands. "I think I'd better speak to my lawyer."

CHAPTER THIRTY SEVEN

1996

Andy Booth was on a rare winning streak. The retired Post Office worker was up fifty pounds on poker night in the Unicorn in Trotterdown.

"What's it to be, Pete?" he said. "You've been staring at those cards for the best part of half a pint.

Pete took his eyes off the cards in his hand and gazed at the pile of money in the middle of the table. There must have been almost a hundred pounds. "All in." He took a wad of notes from his pocket and added it to the pot.

William Landell and James Young, the landlord of the pub looked on eagerly. In all the games of poker they'd played together, this was by far the largest pot any of them had ever played for.

"Show me what you've got," Pete said. "This streak of yours is about to end."

Andy smiled and put a pair of Queens on the table. "And to go with these two beauties are these three." One by one he placed three Kings next to the Queens. "Sorry, Pete. Full House."

William Landell started to clap his hands. "Nice one, Andy. Your time had to come eventually."

"Not too fast," Pete stopped him. "I've also got a couple of royal beauties. Two Dames. But my ladies come with three bullets."

He placed his two Queens and three aces on the pile of money for effect.

"Well I'll be…" Andy Booth's eyes bulged, and he shook his head as Pete scooped up his winnings.

"Nice hand, Pete," William Landell said after the game. "I've only seen aces full once before. "Next round's on you then."

"I think I can manage that," Pete agreed. "Same again?" He addressed the table. Andy Booth nodded. James Young didn't appear to have heard him. He seemed to be deep in thought. It had been two weeks since James' daughter, Jane had been killed. James hadn't been the same since – he'd distanced himself from the world. A temporary manager had been brought in to run the pub and James had increased his alcohol intake dramatically.

"James," Pete said. "Same again?"

James looked across the table. "Make it a triple."

Three or four drinks later, Andy Booth stood up, teetered to the side and quickly steadied himself. "I think I've had enough. Time to face the music. My Martha's going to be furious."

The other three poker players watched as he staggered out the door.

"Poor bastard," Pete said. "I cleaned him out there."

"He'll be back," William Landell said. "One for the road?"

"I'm in," Pete said.

James Young was staring into space again.

"James," Landell said. "Room for another?"

"What?" James' eyes were now half-closed.

"Another drink?"

"Get him another one," Pete said.

William Landell walked up to the bar. "Same again minus Andy's stout."

As he waited for the barman to pour the drinks the telephone behind the bar started to ring. The barman carried on pouring the drinks. The ringing stopped and started up again. The barman scowled, shook his head and answered it. He looked over at William Landell.

"It's for you. It's the wife."

William Landell picked up the phone and shivered. His wife, Lily had never phoned him at the pub before – William worked hard, and Lily wasn't the kind of wife who begrudged him a night out every now and then.

Something was wrong.

"Lily," Landell said. "What's wrong?"

"There's somebody outside the house."

William looked at his watch. It was almost 10. "What do you mean there's someone outside the house?"

"I was upstairs, and I spotted something from the window. It's a man. He's just hanging around outside."

"I'll be there in five minutes."

"William, I think it's that Austrian. He's wearing a red sweater."

William slammed down the handset, ignored the drinks the barman had set down on the counter and returned to his table.

"That bastard is back," he said to Pete and James Young. "Lily phoned and said the Austrian is lingering outside the farmhouse."

James Young seemed to sober up in an instant. His eyes widened, and he stood up. Without saying a word, he made his way towards the exit and went outside.

"I'd better go," Landell said to Pete.

"I'm coming with you."

CHAPTER THIRTY EIGHT

Killian leaned back in his chair in the canteen and stretched his arms behind his back. "I must admit, Pete, I can't make head nor tail of this. I'm reluctant to believe that either of them could kill that French woman."

DS Duncan nodded. "I agree with you, Jack. I've known William Junior since he was a young lad - his wife has a bit of a temper on her but to arrange to meet someone and then kill them beggars belief. What do you want to do now?"

"Wait for Landell's lawyer to get here and then speak to him again. We're going to have to interview the wife though, you realise that."

"I do."

"You've been here a lot longer than me. How well do you know Gilly Landell?"

"Not that well. Her Dad had a pig farm down Grubton way. She got together with William after old man Landell passed away. They only got married a few years ago and she's pretty much kept herself to herself."

"What was Landell senior like? I only met him a few times before he died."

"He was a good man. Hard worker. We used to play poker together once in a while. Family man – William's mother never went without."

Harriet and Eric White came in and sat at the table with Killian and Duncan.

"Any progress?" Harriet asked.

"Not really," Killian replied. "Landell Junior is sticking to his story. He reckons he knows nothing about the text messages on his phone."

"And I suppose there's no way to prove otherwise is there?" Eric said.

"None that I can think of," the DI admitted. "As far as we know the only person who had access to his phone was his wife, Gilly and if she did send the message that implies she knew about the affair."

"It also implies that she sent the message without her husband knowing in order to confront the woman her husband was having an affair with." Duncan added.

"Where's Thomas?" Killian asked.

"I've got him doing a bit of research while he's at a bit of a loose end." Harriet replied.

"Research?"

"I've managed to trace the company that supplied the boots the dead man was wearing."

"Dead man?"

"The one we found in the rocks after Lauren Moreau was found."

"I told you that one is a dead end," Duncan growled.

Killian held up his hand. "Go on, Harriet – what have you found out?"

"The boots were manufactured in the 1990's by a company that called themselves Wanderlust. It was started in the early nineties by Rudolph Schweiss. Schweiss started from his garage and they grew from there. Schweiss was a keen mountaineer and saw a gap in the market for upmarket outdoor clothing and footwear. He managed to obtain funding from a man by the name of Fritz Weidmuller and the company took off."

"Weidmuller?" Duncan exclaimed.

"That's right," Harriet said. "Anyway, I did a bit of digging and discovered that Rudolph Schweiss died in a mountain climbing exhibition in the Andes, but Weidmuller is still alive and well. He ran a successful investment company in Austria until two years ago when he handed over the reins to his son, Alex."

"What are you hoping to gain from this little exercise, DC Taylor?" Duncan asked with obvious sarcasm in his voice.

"I thought if I can get hold of Weidmuller senior, I can find out where these particular hiking boots were sold it might be a start to finding out who this mystery dead man is."

"Waste of time," Duncan scoffed.

"Anyway," Harriet ignored him. "Alex Weidmuller is away in Prague until Monday, so I'll have to wait until then to speak to him about his father but in the meantime, Thomas is probing the internet to see if he can find out about anybody who was reported missing around that time. We're going back a few years here so it's going to take some time."

"Shouldn't we be concentrating all our efforts on the French woman?" Duncan addressed the question to Killian. "Surely that's our main priority?"

"Most of the digging around I've been doing is in my spare time," Harriet defended herself.

Thomas White came in the canteen. "William Landell's lawyer has arrived."

"That was quick," Killian said.

"Apparently he's a local," Thomas said. "Lives in Polgarrow. Landell has another visitor, too. His wife is waiting at the front desk."

"How do you want to play this, Jack?" Duncan asked.

"You and I can speak to Landell again. Harriet, get down to the front desk and see what Gilly Landell is doing here. I've got a feeling this investigation is about to be closed."

* * *

Gilly Landell wasn't in the best of moods when Harriet walked up to her by the front desk. She looked furious.

"What the hell is my husband doing here?" she asked Harriet.

"Mrs Landell," Harriet said calmly. "Would you come through to my office please."

"Answer my question. What is William doing here? And why did I have to find out from one of the farm hands where he went?"

"Please, Mrs Landell, let's go through to my office. Can I get you something to drink?"

"I don't want a drink – I want answers."

"You'll get them," Harriet headed off down the corridor and turned around. "In my office."

Gilly followed her. Harriet opened the door to the room she shared with DS Duncan and beckoned for Gilly to come in.

"Please have a seat," she said, and closed the door.

"Are you going to tell me what the hell is going on here?" Gilly said.

Harriet wasn't sure where to begin. "Your husband is here helping us with our enquiries," she said and realised how ridiculous she sounded.

"What enquiries?" Gilly asked.

"Some new evidence has come to our attention that implicates William in the investigation into the murder of Lauren Moreau."

"What new evidence?"

"I can't go into that right now. Your husband is helping us as we speak. His lawyer has just got here."

"Keith? Why does William need our lawyer?"

"He requested it. Are you sure you don't want something to drink?"

"I want to see my husband. Please can you tell me what's going on here?"

She has no idea, Harriet thought. *Either she's a very good liar or she doesn't know her husband was having an affair.*

Harriet decided that the truth was going to come out in the end, so she decided to take a chance. "Mrs Landell, did you know Lauren Moreau?"

"The French woman who was killed?"

"That's right."

"No. Why are you asking me?"

"Your husband was having an affair with her."

Gilly Landell looked at Harriet as though she'd grown another head. "Are you out of your mind? William? An affair? Who the hell would even look twice at William?"

"I'm afraid it's the truth. It's been going on for a year or so."

"That's the most ridiculous thing I've ever heard. Can I see my husband now?"

"William is being interviewed as we speak, Mrs Landell. I'm afraid this is serious."

Gilly Landell frowned. She looked at Harriet and opened her mouth, but no words came out. She shook her head and suddenly the expression in her eyes changed. It was as though something clicked in her brain. "Do you think William had something to do with the death of that French woman?"

"I'm afraid so," Harriet replied. "I know this is hard but we're going to need to speak to you when my colleagues are finished with your husband. There are some questions that need to be answered."

"William would never cheat on me," Gilly said in a pitiful voice. "We're having a baby for God's sake. He wouldn't do that to me."

Harriet was grateful for the knock on the office door. The door opened, and DI Killian walked in.

"Mrs Landell," Killian said. "Could you come with me, please?"

"Where's William?"

"He's in one of the holding cells," Killian replied. "Please, follow me."
Gilly Landell didn't argue. She stood up and followed the DI out of the office. Harriet walked after them. William Landell came out of Interview room 1 and stood face to face with his wife.
"What have you done?" Gilly asked him.
"It's all a big mistake," William said.
"The only mistake is me marrying you in the first place."
William wasn't expecting the slap that followed. Gilly hit him so hard across the side of the face that Harriet flinched.
"Mrs Landell," Killian said. "That's enough. Please have a seat in there."
He gestured towards the interview room. Gilly did as she was told, and Killian closed the door. William Landell was led back to one of the holding cells by Eric White.

"William Landell still denies sending that text message to Lauren Moreau," Killian told Harriet. "And I believe him."
"His wife doesn't appear to have known about the affair," Harriet said. "She seemed quite genuine."
"Let's see what she has to say then."

CHAPTER THIRTY NINE

An hour later, Killian and Harriet sat in the DI's office. The interview with Gilly Landell hadn't gone well at all. Harriet got the feeling Gilly was genuinely shocked and deeply hurt by her husband's deception.
"She was telling the truth," Killian was on the same page as Harriet. "I don't believe she had a clue about her William's affair."
"I know," Harriet said. "But where does that leave us?"
"William Landell Junior. He's all we have at the moment."
"Do you really think he did it?"
"I don't know what to think anymore. This whole business has got me baffled. Those messages on Landell's phone are pretty incriminating, yet he continues to deny any knowledge of them. I'm knackered, and I can't think straight when I feel like this. I think it's a good idea that we call it a day and approach the whole thing tomorrow with fresh heads."
"What about William Landell?"
"We have more than enough to keep him here. I reckon he's a damn sight safer here than he is at home with his wife anyway."
"You're probably right. I'll see you tomorrow."

DS Duncan was talking to Thomas White by the front desk when Harriet emerged from the corridor. They stopped talking when they spotted her.
"What?" she said. "Are you talking about me?"
"Don't flatter yourself," Duncan said. "What's the deal with William Landell Junior?"
"The DI's called it a day. We'll have another crack at him in the morning."
"It's not yet five," Thomas said.

"I know but we've been banging our heads against a brick wall and it's not doing any good. I agree with the boss – let's see what tomorrow brings. I'll see you in the morning."

"Off to do some more pointless research?" Duncan asked.

"I'm going to get to the bottom of that. You mark my words. I'll see you in the morning."

Harriet drove up to Merryhead. It was still early, and she didn't feel like going straight home. The howling wind was still blowing over the cliff top. Harriet got out the car and stood to face the gusts. She closed her eyes and listened to the sound of the waves crashing over the rocks below. She stood like this until her ears started to sting and she couldn't take any more. She turned and ran back to the car.

On the way home, she thought about the events of the day. *William Landell junior didn't murder Lauren Moreau. What reason did he have to kill her? They were having an affair. Nobody knew about it but William and Lauren.*

The more she thought about it the less it made sense. She pushed the thoughts aside and a picture came into her head. It was the image of the dead body in the rocks – with its tattered clothes and weather-eaten flesh. And a perfectly intact pair of hiking boots. Harriet knew that the origin of those boots was the key to finding out the identification of the owner of the boots. She stopped outside her house, got out the car and ran towards the front door. The wind speed had increased, and the first drops of rain were falling from the sky.

Harriet made her way to the kitchen and made a hot cup of tea. She took it through to the living room and started up her computer. They'd hit a brick wall with the Lauren Moreau investigation but the old corpse in the rocks was a mystery Harriet was determined to solve.

She sipped her tea and looked through her browsing history. She re-read everything again, but nothing jumped out at her.

"There has to be something here."

She took out her phone and dialled Thomas White's number. He answered on the third ring.

"Thomas," Harriet said. "Sorry to bother you after work but with all the chaos at the station I forgot to ask you if you'd managed to dig up anything about the origin of those hiking boots."

"I did find something," Thomas began. "That particular range of boots was only stocked in one store. They were the top of the range at the time and the only place that sold them was an outdoor specialist in Vienna."

"Vienna?" Harriet repeated.

Fritz Weidmuller ran a successful investment company in Vienna.

"The shop in particular closed down in 2001," Thomas continued. "And I couldn't find any details about who owned it. Records from back then seem to be pretty sketchy."

"Tell me about it. Anything else?"

"There's nothing out there to look for, Harriet. The DS is right – I don't think we're going to get any further with this one."

"There has to be something we're missing," Harriet was determined. "And why didn't you mention that particular model was only made in 1996?"

"I must have overlooked it. I'm going to keep looking, anyway. I'll see you tomorrow."

She made another cup of tea and sat back down in front of the computer screen.

"Think, Harriet," she said and typed in Fritz Weidmuller in the search bar for the tenth time. She looked past the first two pages and scanned the third one. Something caught her eye. She clicked on the link and a newspaper article appeared on the screen. The article was from 1996. There was a photograph of Fritz Weidmuller. Two young men were standing on either side of him. They didn't look much older than nineteen or twenty. Harriet read the caption. The young men were Fritz Weidmuller's sons, Alex and Jurgen.

"He had another son," she said out loud.

She read the article. Weidmuller and his sons had just returned from climbing the north face of The Eiger. They'd done it in record time. Harriet looked at the photograph again. Her eyes focused on the clothing the three men were wearing – especially their boots. She looked more closely but image was too blurred. She right clicked on the photograph, saved it and opened it up in her pictures. She zoomed in on the boots.

"Wanderlust Mark 4," she said. "If I'm not mistaken. Four thousand Deutsche Marks a pair."

Her heart started to beat faster but then slowed down when she realised something.

Fritz Weidmuller had a stake in the company at the time. Why is it so unusual that he and his sons would be wearing that brand of hiking boot?

Harriet switched off her computer, took a sip of tea and winced. The tea had gone cold. There was a knock at the door. She was surprised – she wasn't expecting anybody, and she rarely had visitors turn up unannounced. She turned off the computer monitor and walked down the hallway to the front door.

DS Duncan was standing on the step when Harriet opened the door. He was holding a half-full bottle of whisky. Harriet could smell the booze on him straight away.

"Can I come in?" he asked. "It's bloody Baltic out here."
"Of course. Come inside. Can I get you something to drink?
Duncan held out the bottle. "Just a glass, thanks."

Harriet made some more tea and she and Duncan sat opposite each other in the living room. Duncan swigged down a full glass of whisky and filled another right to the brim.
"I'm sorry to come round unannounced," he slurred. "But I think there's something you need to know. It's about this obsession of yours with a 21-year-old corpse."
"21-year-old?" Harriet was shocked. Why had the DS said twenty-one-year old?

"Before I begin," Duncan said. "You need to understand something. I know I should have said something earlier, but I was scared. Scared shitless. If this gets out, my career – my whole life is over."
"I don't understand. If what gets out?"
"Just listen. You can make your mind up what to do when I'm finished."

CHAPTER FORTY

1996

William Landell and Pete Duncan stood outside the Unicorn in Trotterdown and watched as James Young sped off in his car. Landell winced as James's car took the wing mirror off a parked car as he careered down the road.
"We'd better get after him," Duncan said. "If it is the Austrian at your place, I dread to think what James will do once he gets hold of him."
They got inside Landell's Land Rover and headed off in the direction of the farm.
"What the hell is he doing at the farm anyway?" Landell asked.
"Maybe it's not him," Duncan suggested. "It's dark out – maybe Lily was mistaken."
"She didn't sound mistaken. She sounded scared if you ask me."
   They reached the farm five minutes later. James Young's car was parked outside the house, but James was nowhere to be seen. Landell and Duncan got out and ran inside the farm house. Lily was standing in the hallway holding onto William Junior.
"Where's James?" Landell asked his wife.
"He came in, asked where the man was last seen and ran straight out when I told him," Lily replied.
"Where was this?" Duncan asked. "Where did you last see him?"
"He was just past the old barn. Just standing there he was. Like he was up to no good."
"Lock the door behind us," Landell ordered. "And don't answer the door to anyone but us. Come on, Pete."

Duncan and Landell headed off in the direction of the old barn. The moon was full, so they could see quite clearly in the darkness. They found James Young a few hundred metres up ahead. He was sitting on the grass with his head in his hands. The light of the moon shone down on his hands. They were covered in blood.

"James," Landell said. "Are you alright? What happened?"

James didn't move. He carried on staring at the blood on his hands.

"What happened to your hands, James?" Duncan asked.

"He's over there," James gestured with his head in the direction of the fence that surrounded the farm.

Duncan turned to look. There was something on the ground near the fence. He got closer and realised what it was. A man wearing a red sweater was lying face down on the grass. As Duncan got closer he spotted the blood on his head. He felt for a pulse but there was nothing – the man was dead. Duncan walked back to James and William Landell.

"What happened, James?"

"I spotted him as soon as I got outside the farm house," James told him in a voice little more than a whisper. "I caught up to him. I asked him what the hell he was doing there?"

"What was he doing here?" Landell asked.

"He didn't reply. He turned and looked at me and then he smiled. Can you believe it? The bastard smiled at me. That was when I socked him one. I didn't hit him hard enough. He swung back at me and his fist connected with my chin. All the time he was smiling."

"What did you do to him, James?" Duncan asked.

"He told me my daughter was very pretty. Can you believe it? He said it in his fucking German accent – 'you had a very pretty daughter'.

Then he took out a knife and sniffed the blade like it was a fine perfume."

James started to shake. He was shivering all over. Duncan put his hand on his shoulder, but James shrugged him off.

"He said he could still smell Jane's blood on the blade, Pete. That's what he said, like it was nothing. Then he moved towards me with the knife in his hand. That bastard killed my little girl. There was a rock next to my foot, so I picked it up and flung it at him as hard as I could. It was a big rock. I got a lucky shot – it hit him square in the forehead. He dropped the knife and I moved in. I hit him over and over again with the rock. I hit him until I had nothing left inside me and then I hit him again. I killed him, Pete."

None of them spoke a word for a while.

"It was self-defence," William Landell said eventually. "He had a knife. He killed your daughter, for Christ sakes." He looked to Duncan for verification. "What do you say, Pete. It was self-defence."

"I don't know, William. This doesn't look like self-defence." He turned to James. "How many times did you hit him?"

"I don't know," James was still shaking. "Fifteen, maybe twenty."

"You killed him. You kept on hitting him even when he was man down. This doesn't look good."

"The bastard killed his daughter. He taunted him with that fact. Come on, Pete – you'd have done the same."

"I need to think," Duncan said. "This is bad." He looked over at the lifeless body on the ground. "We need to get rid of the body."

"You can't be serious," Landell exclaimed.

"We need to get rid of the body," Duncan said once more. "Nobody can know what happened here tonight. If this gets out, James is going to go down for murder. You tell Lily whoever she saw is long gone."

"But, Pete."

"Have you got that? This never happened. Now help me find somewhere to dump him."

Duncan and Landell grabbed a leg each and dragged the lifeless body to a group of rocks next to a cluster of small trees. Duncan searched the man's clothes and found a wallet and a passport. "Jurgen Weidmuller," he said and stuffed the wallet and passport in his pocket. "I'm burning these as soon as I have a chance."

He and Landell forced the young Austrian through a gap in the rocks until he was completely out of sight.

"That ought to be deep enough," Duncan said. "The elements will get rid of him sooner or later. This night never happened. Do I make myself clear?"

Landell and James Young both nodded in agreement.

"Nobody will ever know," Duncan added.

CHAPTER FORTY ONE

"Nobody will ever know," Duncan filled up his glass.
The bottle was almost empty.
"Oh my God," Harriet said.
"So, now *you* know. Are you happy now?"
"Jurgen Weidmuller? He was Fritz Weidmuller's son. I've been so close all along. I was going to try and find the dead man's father on Monday."
"Was?"
"I mean I am. I don't know what I'm going to do. Why the hell did you bury the body? James Young wouldn't have been convicted for murder – there were extenuating circumstances. Weidmuller killed his daughter. He had a knife."
"We couldn't take the risk. That arrogant Austrian had a rich, powerful father – do you really think he would have let James get away with killing his son?"
"I can't take all of this in. You're a police officer. You were a police officer back then. How could you dispose of a body?"
"I thought of nothing else for weeks afterwards, believe you me, but it was the only thing we could have done under the circumstances. Jurgen Weidmuller got what he deserved – I realised that in the end."
"No," Harriet said, much louder than she intended. "That's how you justified it. It still doesn't make it right. You were a representative of the law. Doesn't that mean anything?"
"Don't be so naïve, Harriet. Sometimes the law isn't all black and white. This was one of those grey areas. What do you think the alternatives were? Report it to the police? Sit back and watch as

James's life got destroyed? Don't you think the man had been through enough already?"

"He killed a man in cold blood," Harriet reminded him.

"Don't you think I know that?"

"What are you going to do?" Duncan asked.

"I don't know. I really don't know. Why the hell did you come here tonight?"

"You were so obsessed with this. I came to give you what you wanted."

"21 years," Harriet said. "You've carried this with you for all that time. Weren't you scared that it would get out? That somebody would find out what you'd done?"

"William Landell, James Young and me made a deal that night," Duncan told her. "We promised to never again mention what we did that night and it was never mentioned."

"21 years," Harriet said again. "That was some deal you made. Some secret."

"A secret that only I know about."

"And me, now."

"And you. Old Landell took it with him to his grave, as did James Young."

"James Young is dead?"

"He couldn't take any more. Hung himself from the rafters of the Unicorn a few years after that night."

"The Unicorn?" Harriet couldn't believe what she was hearing.

"There's a few things you're yet to learn about this part of the world, Harriet."

"Why are you telling me all of this?" Harriet asked.

"Why do you think? You were about to get in touch with the father of the man we buried under the rocks 21 years ago. Don't you think he'd put two and two together and realise his son was in this part of the world at that time. It would have opened up a can of worms." Duncan poured what was left of the whisky into his glass. "The old man's loaded, Harriet – he would've done everything in his power to get to the truth, and then my life would be over."

"We can't just bury this."

"It's been buried for over 20 years. Leave it there." Duncan finished what was left in his glass. "I've told you what happened. Now it's up to you what to do with that information. I'll see you at work tomorrow. I'll see myself out."

Harriet sat staring at the wall opposite her for ages when Duncan had gone. She was finding it hard to take in what the DS had just told her.

How could they just get rid of the body? She thought. *How could a police officer be involved in something like that?*

She made some more tea and sipped it slowly. The information she was now privy to was too much for her. She picked up her phone and dialled a number.

"Jon," Dr Finch answered immediately. "What are you up to tonight?" Harriet hoped that Finch wasn't in bed already.

"Just settling down to watch a riveting documentary about the sexual behaviour of dolphins," Finch replied. "Why do you ask?"

"I need to talk to somebody. I need to talk to you."

"Where are you?"

"At home."

"Is everything alright?"

"Yes. I mean no. Can you come over?"

"I'll be there in ten minutes."

Harriet put down her phone and wondered if she'd done the right thing. She knew she could trust Jon Finch, but she didn't know how much she could trust him. DS Duncan's bombshell was already feeling like a heavy weight around her neck, and she needed another opinion as to what to do with what she now knew.

The ten minutes before Finch knocked on the door seemed to take forever. Harriet sat watching the clock on the wall the whole time, and when she heard the knock she jumped. She rushed to the door and opened it.

"What's wrong?" Finch asked.

"Come in," Harriet said. "Can I get you something to drink?"

"Coffee would be great. What's going on, Harriet? You've got me worried."

They went through to the kitchen and Harriet made coffee and a fresh cup of tea for herself. They sat down at the kitchen table.

"I'm sorry to drag you out like this," Harriet said. "But I don't know who else to talk to."

"Just tell me what's wrong. You're starting to freak me out."

Harriet told him what DS Duncan had told her. Finch listened to the whole thing without saying a word.

"I don't know what to do," Harriet said when she was finished. "They buried the body. How could they do that?"

"Hmm," Finch said. "This is a tricky one. What are you planning on doing with this information?"

"I don't know. That's why I asked you to come round. I really don't know what to do. If this gets out, Duncan's career is over – he could even end up in jail and, despite what he did, I don't want that."

"There's your answer then. I don't approve of what they did – killing a man and burying him away for all these years is despicable, but you have to admit the circumstances were exceptional. The man killed a young girl. Her father acted in a way that most fathers would have acted. I don't have children, but I reckon losing a child like that must be the worst thing in the world. The man was still mourning the death of his girl when he came face to face with her killer."

"What do you suggest I do?" Harriet said.

"Leave it be. Keep it buried. No good will come of bringing the whole mess up again."

"They killed a man and hid his body."

"It was 21 years ago, Harriet. And from what I've heard, the man deserved everything he got. Think of it this way – if you let this get out you'll be opening a Pandora's Box. It'll not only be DS Duncan who'll have his head on the chopping board, the Trotterdown police force will be torn apart. The press will have a field day."

Harriet thought about what Jon Finch had said but she was still not sure what to do. It was a moral issue. She still could not condone what Duncan had been a part of. He was an officer of the law at the time and he kept a cold-blooded murder quiet.

"It's the only way, Harriet." Finch said calmly. "You know it is. The man was a killer. He got what he deserved."

"I'll sleep on it," Harriet said even though she knew full well that sleep was out of the question – there were too many thoughts running through her head.

Finch finished his coffee. "I'd better get going. I've got an early start in the morning. I want to go down and check on the boat – these gales we've been having can wreak havoc on the rigging." He kissed Harriet on the cheek. "Let this thing go. Like I said, no good will come from bringing it up again."

CHAPTER FORTY TWO

Harriet did manage to sleep that night, but it was only after lying awake until 2 in the morning, staring into space, that she gave in and popped two of the blue pills into her mouth. Within ten minutes the numbness spread, and darkness followed. She regretted her decision when her alarm clock woke her five hours later. Her head was throbbing, and her muscles felt lame. She forced herself to get out of bed and went downstairs to make some tea. The wind was rattling the windows and drops of rain were starting to fall.

"Why did I take those bloody pills?" Harriet said to her cup of tea.
She thought about what Jon Finch had said the night before.
No good will come from bringing it up again.
Harriet knew he was right of course, but she still wasn't sure what to do. She didn't want to see DS Duncan lose everything – Duncan could be a bit of a pain at times, but deep down he was OK. She decided she would try and put the whole thing out of her mind. She finished the tea and went back upstairs to prepare herself for the day ahead.

* * *

Nothing Harriet could have done would have prepared her for the scene that met her as she walked into the station in Trotterdown. Gilly Landell was screaming at Eric White by the front desk.
"I demand to see my husband!" she bellowed. "I'm not leaving until you let me see the cheating bastard."
Harriet approached the desk. "Mrs Landell, please calm down. Let's go up to the canteen and have a cup of tea."
"Don't you tell me to calm down. I want to see that scheming wretch husband of mine."

"I'll see if we can arrange something. But first you need to calm down."

"I want to tell him it's over. Finished. That's all. Then you can do what you like to the two-timing bastard."

DI Killian walked in with DS Duncan. Duncan looked terrible – his eyes were puffy and bloodshot, and he was badly in need of a shave. "Morning," Killian said. He spotted Gilly Landell. "Is everything alright?"

"Mrs Landell wants to see her husband," Harriet told him.

"I'm sure that won't be a problem," Killian said. "Please take a seat and I'll let him know you're here."

The DI walked off down the corridor before Gilly Landell had a chance to say anything further.

"Harriet," Duncan said. "Can I have a word?"

Harriet followed him to the canteen and they sat at a table next to the window.

"I need to know," Duncan said. "I need to know what you're going to do about what we spoke of last night. I have to prepare myself."

"I still don't know what to do," Harriet admitted. "Part of me wants to see justice take its course but the other part of me wants to leave it in the past."

"Justice? Where's the justice in a young girl having her life taken away from her like that. You tell me where's the justice in that?"

"I don't want to see you in trouble, but I'm not sure how I can live with myself knowing what you did. Jon Finch told me to let it lie."

Duncan frowned. "What the hell has Finch got to do with this?"

"I needed someone to talk to. You dumped quite a lot on me last night and I just needed somebody else's opinion."

"You should listen to that boyfriend of yours. He's right – let it lie."

"I still need some time to think it over. We should be getting back to work. I think William Landell Junior is going to need some protection from that wife of his."

Killian sat opposite William Landell Junior in one of the interview rooms. William's wife sat next to the DI. Killian had managed to get her to calm down.

"How could you?" she said. "How could you do this? We have a baby on the way."

William's mouth opened but no words came out.

"Don't you have anything to say? You coward."

"I'm sorry," William said eventually. "It just happened."

"It just happened? Well, let me tell you what's going to happen now. We're finished – I'm through with you and your lies and I'm going to let you rot in jail. You deserve everything that's coming to you."

"I didn't kill her," William pleaded. "I didn't kill Lauren."

Gilly Landell stood up and before Killian could stop her she slapped her husband on the face so hard that the DI flinched.

"Lauren?" she shouted. "Precious Lauren. Well, you can join her in the ground for all I care."

She raised her hand again, but this time Killian was quick enough. He gripped the hand. "Gilly, that's enough. I think you'd better leave."

"I'm going." She glared at her husband. "I hope they nail your balls to the wall, you two-timing bastard."

Gilly Landell stormed past Harriet and Eric at the reception desk and headed for the door. She opened it and stood face to face with Donovan Beech. The experienced farm hand looked awful. His face was pale, and he had heavy bags under his eyes.

"What are you doing here?" Gilly asked him. "I suppose you're taking that bastard husband of mine's side on this one."

"No, Gilly," Beech said quietly. "That's not why I'm here." He turned to Harriet. "We need to talk."

"What's going on?" she asked him.

"Not here."

"We can talk in one of the interview rooms. Come with me."

They sat down in the room William Landell Junior had just vacated. "What's going on, Mr Beech?" Harriet asked.

"I heard that Mr Landell was here. That he's going down for the murder of that French woman."

"I can't talk about that."

"William's not a bad lad. He's made his mistakes and now he's paying for them. His wife might take him back, but his life is going to be hell for a while."

"Where are you going with this?" Harriet asked.

"William didn't kill that woman. He was seeing her on the side but that's as far as it went. He didn't kill her."

"How do you know all this?"

"It wasn't supposed to happen. If I could go back in time I would. I can't see young William go down for something he didn't do."

"What are you trying to tell me, Mr Beech?"

CHAPTER FORTY THREE

One week earlier

Donovan Beech had found out about the affair William Landell Junior was having with Lauren Moreau a few months earlier. William had been careless – his wife had been away for a weekend visiting her sister and William had used the opportunity to spend a few hours with his lover. Beech knew straight away what was going on, but he kept quiet. It was none of his business. When Lauren Moreau had come back to town a month later and Beech spotted William and her together again, he'd decided to intervene. Gilly was pregnant, and Beech thought enough was enough. He'd approached William but had been told to mind his own business.

Now, the French woman was back, and Beech decided it was time to warn her off once and for all. He found William Landell Junior's phone on the kitchen table while he was there having his first early-morning cup of coffee. William left the room and an idea came to Beech. He opened up the phone and sent a message to the French woman.

Just before 8, Beech set off. He couldn't stand by and watch as William Landell Junior ruined his and his wife's life – the affair had to end. He turned left onto the dirt road that led to the edge of Landell's Farm and carried on for another five minutes until he reached the part that almost met up with the coast-to-coast trail.

He spotted her when she was about a hundred metres away. She was walking towards him briskly. He got out of the car and started walking up to her. She saw him, but she carried on walking.

"You need to stay away from William," Beech said.

"And you need to mind your own business. What are *you* doing here? I'm here to meet William."

"You're here to wreck lives. It has to stop right now."

She started to laugh, and something snapped in Donovan Beech. He grabbed her arm and pulled her towards him. "Do I have to spell it out for you? It ends now. Have you got that?"

"You're hurting me." Lauren managed to break free from Beech's grasp and started to run.

Beech ran after her. He was very fit for his age, and he soon started to gain ground. Lauren turned around, saw Beech getting closer and removed her rucksack from her back. She threw it into the bushes by the side of the path as she ran. It was no use. Beech was getting closer. She increased her pace but so did the middle-aged farm hand. Beech was now only about five metres behind her and showing no sign of slowing down.

He caught up to her fifty metres later. He barged into her and she fell to the ground in a heap. She tried to get up, but Beech was already on her.

"This is your last chance," he said, out of breath.

"You're crazy. You attacked me. I'm going to the police."

Beech found a rock on the ground and picked it up. "You're not going anywhere." He swung the rock and hit her on the back of the head. Lauren winced in pain and put her hand to her injured head. Beech hit her again and again. The rock was now covered in blood. Lauren Moreau lay on her side on the ground. She wasn't moving.

Beech looked around him. The smoke coming out of the chimney in the farmhouse was visible in the distance. He grabbed hold of Lauren Moreau's feet and dragged her towards a rocky outcrop fifty metres away. He placed her body on the ground next to the rocks and covered it with some dead branches and leaves. He put the rock he'd killed her with in his jacket pocket and headed back towards his car, not realising that Lauren Moreau was still alive.

CHAPTER FORTY FOUR

"He confessed?" Killian said. "Donovan Beech confessed to the murder of Lauren Moreau?"

The DI was in his office. Harriet and DS Duncan sat opposite him.

"Do you think he's telling the truth?" Killian added.

"Yes," Harriet replied. "He brought in the rock he used to kill her. Forensics have it right now, but I bet you Lauren Moreau's blood will be all over it."

"Why did he do it?" Duncan asked. "Why did he have to kill her?"

"He says he was looking out for the Landells," Harriet explained. "He couldn't stand by and watch a family get ripped apart. He said he didn't mean to kill her – he just lost it for a while and went too far. He reckoned he couldn't stop himself."

"But why confess?" Duncan said. "We'd cleared him from the investigation. He would have got away with it."

"Donovan Beech has a conscience," Harriet said. "I'd never have expected it of him – I mean, he comes across as an arrogant, grumpy old man but he couldn't stand by and watch William Landell Junior get sent to prison for something he didn't do. You have to respect him for that."

"He killed a woman in cold blood," Killian pointed out. "I have no respect for a man who can do that. No matter what the circumstances. A murder is a murder."

Harriet glanced across at DS Duncan. She noticed he was rather fidgety – he was tugging at a button on his shirt.

"Well then," Killian said. "We'll wait to see what Littlemore and his team have to say about the rock, but I'd say this one's over. Now we can start with the other body. See if we can satisfy that curiosity of yours, Harriet."

DS Duncan twisted the button in his hand so hard that it popped off and flew across the room.

"I've been thinking about that," Harriet said and looked at Duncan. "I'm starting to think that one's a dead end. The DS was right all along – it was probably just some old tramp who took shelter from the cold and froze to death in the process. Accidental death."

"Accidental death," Killian agreed.

THE END

Detective Harriet Taylor series

 THE BEEKEEPER — STEWART GILES	Alice Green is a beekeeper in the small Cornish village of Polgarrow. She lives with her pet jackdaw in a beautiful cottage not far from the sea. One evening, Alice finds something strange under the hollyhock bush in her garden. The gruesome discovery will change everyone's lives. And then Alice's best friend Milly disappears . . . Detective Harriet Taylor has just transferred to the area from Edinburgh. As she investigates a series of shocking crimes, she grows close to the old beekeeper and is determined to bring the criminals to justice. But who is really what they seem and who can she trust? A crime mystery with a touch of black humour.
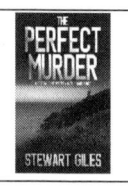 THE PERFECT MURDER — STEWART GILES	Two cats are found mutilated in the same town. Detective Harriet Taylor is reluctant to investigate, but then one of their owners is killed a bizarre way that same day. Harriet and the team step in. The dead woman has four words written on her neck — four very ambiguous words. Then another body turns up with the same words written on it. Harriet fears the worst — a serial killer is on the loose in the small Cornish town of Trotterdown.

DS Jason Smith series

 PHOBIA — Stewart Giles	Phobia is a series of five DS Jason Smith cases he worked on before we met him in the first book 'Smith'. We get insights into what moulded him into the Detective Sergeant we first get a glimpse of in 'Smith'. Smith quickly realizes that police work isn't always cut and dry. Justice is not always black and white; there are many shades of grey in between.

 SMITH Stewart Giles	It is Christmas Day in York. A woman is found dead in her bed. A suicide note is found on her chest. It reads 'I am so sorry Martin'. Hours later the police are called to a house a few miles away. A mother and her daughter have been brutally attacked; the mother is dead and the daughter is barely alive.
 Boomerang Stewart Giles	A man is killing people in York. Initially the murders appear to be the random acts of a maniac. Detective Jason Smith is put in charge of the investigation. It soon becomes clear that the murders are all connected to him in one way or another. All of the killings correspond to events in Smith's life and the murderer leaves dates at the crime scene which tie up to important dates in Smith's history.
 LADYBIRD	Detective Sergeant Jason Smith is days away from the end of his sick leave after a case that almost cost him his life when he gets a call from an old friend. His friend has been arrested for the murder of a student. He wants Smith to investigate the murder and prove his innocence. Smith is persuaded return to work. The student was killed with a bread knife. Ladybirds were scattered on his dead body. When another man is found dead with ladybirds scattered on his body Smith and his team are baffled. That is until they unearth a sinister secret from 20 years earlier. Somebody wants revenge and Smith must act fast to find out the truth.
 OCCAM'S RAZOR STEWART GILES	A football player is shot dead in front of a packed crowd of people. DS Jason Smith is put in charge of the investigation. The murder weapon is found in a house across the road from the football ground. It is a rare Russian army issue sniper rifle. As the investigation hits dead end after dead end, two government agents arrive and take over, pushing Smith and his colleagues to the side. As more people die, Smith realises that these people are not who they appear to be. He is forced into the dark world of these 'phantoms' and finds himself at the mercy of his nemesis – the man who kidnapped his sister many years earlier.
 Harlequin Stewart Giles	The circus comes to town and children start to disappear. Detective Sergeant Jason Smith is persuaded to return to work after three weeks of a marijuana induced haze. Forced to endure the leadership of a new DI, the fulsome Bryony Brownhill, Smith is faced with the most difficult investigation of his colourful career. When the children who vanished are found murdered in various parts of the city, all clues lead to the circus grounds but Smith and his team are met with a sinister silence everywhere they turn.

SELENE Stewart Giles	When a man is found tucked up in bed with his throat sliced open two days after Christmas, DS Jason Smith and his team are baffled. It appears he has been drugged, killed and carefully wrapped up in a duvet. The only evidence Smith finds are some strands of hair belonging to a woman. One month later, another man is killed in exactly the same manner but there appears to be no link whatsoever to the two men apart from the fact that they were both single, lonely and middle aged. In the midst of the coldest winter in years, Smith and his team run out of ideas and the tension mounts. The only clue they have is the murders were carried out under the light of the full moon. Haunted by lucid dreams and double awakenings, Smith stumbles upon something that will send him on the hunt for the most terrifying murderer he has ever come across.
HORSEMEN STEWART GILES	One draining murder investigation after another has left DS Jason on the brink of losing his sanity and he needs a break. A string of armed robberies at the McDonalds in the city of York are getting in the way. Smith's DI makes him a deal; if he can get to the bottom of it, he can have two weeks off. Smith figures out who the brains behind the robberies is; the young wife of Jimmy Phoenix, the owner of all the McDonalds franchises in the city. Smith sets off to the peaceful Yorkshire village of Scarpdale intending to forget about everything – slow walks by the lakes and no phone reception. Things take a turn for the worse when he wakes up on his first morning to find 3 policemen banging on his door. A young woman has been murdered. Smith was the last person to speak to her.
UNWORTHY STEWART GILES	DS Jason Smith is dragged away from paternity leave when a woman is killed with her baby in the next room. When more women with children are brutally murdered, Smith discovers that they all have something in common - they all share a secret. When he finds out that the mother of his own child is on this list of 'Unworthy' women, he finds himself in a race against time to stop the killer before his whole world comes crashing down around him.

I hope you've enjoyed reading. Please leave a review on Amazon or you can contact me on starmarine@polka.co.za to give me any feedback. I will reply to all correspondence.

Printed in Poland
by Amazon Fulfillment
Poland Sp. z o.o., Wrocław